Smoke On The Cruise

Shields and Shadows, Volume 2

Preston Olson

Published by Preston Olson, 2024.

SMOKE ON THE CRUISE

First edition. January 19, 2024.

ISBN: 979-8224174348

Written by Preston Olson.

Table of Contents

Chapter One: Morning Rush

"Do you see anyone inside?" Detective Reisen inquires.

"Five guys playing cards," Detective Dewalt whispers.

"Where is our target?"

Detective Dewalt peers closer, "Losing, harshly."

Against a brick building, Detectives Reisen, and Dewalt are prepared to execute a search warrant. Bushes and shrubbery around the house keep them shielded from the street. Both detectives are unseen by any watchful eyes.

"Are you ready to save the taxpayers money?"

"Only if your nutty idea works," Detective Dewalt says.

Detective Reisen knocks, "Vance Magowski, we have legal authorization to search your premises. Please, conduct yourself in a properly manner and come outside with your hands up."

Hearing no response, they kick open the door. Four men stand up with weapons drawn. Before they can fire off a shot, Detectives Reisen, and Dewalt fill the aggressors full of hot smoking lead.

Doors swing open as Detectives Reisen and Dewalt haul in Vance Magowski, for fingerprinting at the precinct. One of the largest kingpins in Chicago has been caught in a large-scale drug trafficking scheme—the biggest bust by Progressive Task Force 12-Z, or any department this year.

Curtains with navy blue drapes capture cool air inside. Sunshine beams down as morning arrives.

"Whoa! We are running late!" Detective Reisen shouts.

"One minute! One more minute!" Bonnie yells.

Our flight departs in less than an hour. Nothing pauses Bonnie while watering flowers. Wishing for a way to freeze time frames. Nothing goes the right way when you have zero time to waste.

"A woman must be proper," she maintains.

"I don't remember a day when you weren't."

Fetching our belongings while our love is revolving. Driving a short distance without counting minutes. Long narrow lines of people standing at a distance. Waves blasting off rocks that are durable, and rigid. What started in the kitchen is fully baked into a vision. A day producing beautiful weather promotes hope. No room for a mope or a passenger boat.

"Good morning! My name is Charlene, representing Big Nebula Airlines! I will be overjoyed to assist you today with your flying needs."

"We have two tickets for Tampa Bay, Florida," Detective Reisen announces.

Detective Reisen sets both tickets on the desk in front of Charlene.

"This will only take a few moments," she reassures.

Charlene checks each ticket into the computer system. Detective Reisen and Bonnie absorb the room's ambiance.

"Here you are," Charlene begins.

Passing the tickets back to us, "Flight 201 is your dream getaway! Thank you both for flying with Big Nebula Airlines! Please, enjoy your flight!"

"Thank you," Detective Reisen replies.

"We appreciate you," Bonnie chimes in.

Picking up our pace after checking out of baggage claim. Off in the distance could be rain. Carrying a load of luggage as we board the plane. Escorting Bonnie to her seat before storing our suitcases overhead. Wouldn't be surprised if I head back to bed, and then wake up to clonk my head.

"Won't take long until we land. I am going to get some quick shut-eye."

"Do you believe former Mayor Riley is getting any shut-eye?" Bonnie inquires.

"Heard she hired an expensive attorney," Reisen replies.

"Will that be enough to save her skin?" Bonnie probes.

"I wouldn't be shocked. Don't lose any sleep over it."

Kissing Bonnie before curling up against the window. Snug as a bug until I nod off into a dream world. Not too long has gone by before feeling a tap on my arm. Bonnie acts as an alarm from time to time.

"Are we in Tampa Bay?"

"If not, this simulation is lifelike," she quips.

"Anything is better than the simulation we left."

Bonnie slips in a kiss as I rise to grab our luggage. All that lay on my mind is purchasing grub. Moshing through the airport lobby.

"Are you hungry?"

"Starving!" Bonnie shouts.

"This is uplifting news. I was prepared to eat for you."

"We could wait, and eat on the cruise," she contends.

"I will walk the plank before boarding a ship hungry."

"How dramatic," she scoffs. "You were certainly rushing me. Your appetite remains a mystery!"

"Stick around, my appetite has a story of its own."

"You are the one that's stuck," Bonnie relishes.

Grabbing my hand as we move step-by-step. Reaching the counter of a dive restaurant named Curly's Fryer. Glossing over the menu as I sense Bonnie following suit.

At the service counter is a man with an old-school paper boat hat on.

"Hey, I'm Curly. Are you ready to order?"

"Tenderloin! Make it extra crispy with the works."

"Chili cheese dog and a half-pound of French fries."

"Sure, is a boatload of French fries," Detective Reisen says.

"Covered in extra goodness for you, and I."

"Coming right up. Do you want any drinks?" Curly asks.

"You are a mind reader." Glancing at Bonnie and giving her a peck on the lips. "Two medium-size fountain drinks to go with our order, please," Detective Reisen responds.

"Two big drinks coming at you!" Curly blurts.

Dropping one tenderloin, and a humongous basket of French fries into the deep fryer. Curly begins making Bonnie's chili cheese dog. Curly's Dive Restaurant has a nostalgic vibe.

"We need a vacation more often," Detective Reisen suggests.

Leaning in fast before kissing Bonnie gently on the neck—while taking in her aroma. Apple Orchard scents, with subtle hints of Wildflowers, overpower burgers, and onions.

"Are you dining inside, or do I bag it?" Curly asks.

Snatching me from my rather wild fantasies.

"No, sir. Taking the food to go," Detective Reisen requests.

A professional cooking our food means each bite must be delectable. Paying for our meals with fresh greenbacks. Grabbing napkins, and sauces out of a small dish.

"Order up!" Curly shouts.

Passing us our food with a sigh of relief. Both bags smell better than any meal deal in weeks. Sneaking in a few bites while heading for the exit. The beef is delicious and labeled nutritious. Made with love, and fresh lettuce.

Stepping outside and hailing a taxi. Couldn't have gone better than how I first pictured it. Fitting our luggage in the trunk. Bonnie situates herself inside of the cab.

"We are heading for a cruise," Reisen proclaims.

In the driver's seat is a man sporting blue glasses. Thick brown bushy eyebrows quenching above. A doughy face, and a round body. Listening to oldies radio, the song is called, 'Oh, My Lordy.'

"Call me, Amsted. The entrance to the ports is blocked for a few hours due to construction."

"Bring us closer than here, please," Reisen decides.

Sensing Bonnie stare without hearing a sound.

"How do you plan on getting us there?"

"Working on it. When we are closer, I will know."

Chapter Two: Steep Sharp Hearts

Detective Reisen, and Bonnie make headway as their relationship makes waves. Lightning strikes far out over the bay. Intense winds back in Chicago obliterate the fray. The stage feels set for passion and excitement. Trusting in an alternative way. An appointment awaits at a port out of the way. Hard to say, what is more important at the present moment. Won't make a difference if Detective Reisen is timely and focused down by the ocean.

"Do you mind if we finish our food back here?"

Amsted glares at Detective Reisen through the rear-view mirror before a smirk appears.

"I don't mind, as long as you don't spill all over the place."

"Thank you, kindly. We promise not to make a mess," Bonnie replies.

Nearing the port—noticing a traffic jam. Seeing the cruise ship dead ahead, "Pull over on the shoulder up ahead."

"Is your plan cooking?" Bonnie inquires.

"Let's hope I don't burn the main course."

Amsted parks in a neatly tucked away available spot.

"Here you are good, sir," Detective Reisen states.

Paying the cab fare and leaving a hefty tip.

"Thank you, friend. Take excellent care of yourselves," Amsted encourages.

"We will. Thank you for the lift," Bonnie replies.

"I will grab our luggage, sweetheart," Reisen suggests.

Sliding around the taxicab. Opening Bonnie's door and helping her out. Amsted presses a button to open the trunk.

"Shut the trunk when you are done, please."

Empty our luggage on the sidewalk. Mainly the many belongings of Bonnie.

"Thank, God, you packed light."

"I see the cruise ship. How do you see us boarding?"

The cruise ship's entrance is layered by a tall fence, with a few mossy knolls on the other side. A sidewalk stops at the end of the road where a traffic jam holds up everyone's day. There is no way around this mess. A theory could hypothetically become a test. If succeeding proves any-thing then failing is worth a chance.

Climbing on top of a concrete ledge. Carefully dropping our be-longings over the fence.

"Some master plan," Bonnie gripes.

"Wait until you see the grand finale!"

Tossing over the last bit of luggage before hurling himself over the fence. Splat! Landing square in the mud.

"This is a mess! We are unorganized!" Bonnie howls.

Detective Reisen pulls himself out of the muck.

"No foul play suspected," he says, before falling back in.

"You cannot expect me to climb over. Do you really?"

"Don't be afraid. I will guide you down once you climb up. Can't have both of us putting on sludge monster costumes."

Bonnie climbs up the fence. Detective Reisen helps her down to the other side. They kiss for a few moments. Collecting their gear, and quickly reorganizing. Even in humiliating moments, Bonnie shows candor and unlimited composure.

Walking down a narrow path between a retention pond, and a gat-ed fence.

"What are you getting into?" Bonnie inquires.

"What holds something together, but keeps someone out?"

"I don't understand your riddle."

Past the muddy patch is a gate leading out.

"A latch!"

"Way too early for this type of behavior from you!"

Bonnie pulls her suitcase on wheels out of the thick grass. Trekking toward the cruise ship step for step. Dragging important belongings along the asphalt. Any other item rests around their backs and sides.

"How did all of these folks find a way here without falling in the mud?"

Bonnie points, "Maybe, a different sidewalk."

People congregate around displays containing tourist information. Other folks board the cruise ship with no hesitation. A band is playing charming tunes as people take pictures near them. Overtaken by good music, the atmosphere is amazing.

A few odd couples fill in along concrete slab benches. Absorbing a glorious view anyone would be blessed to see. An encapsulating purple, fluorescent skyline, with orange shading above. Clouds glide swiftly, changing colors, and shifting. A road to paradise has never felt so tempting.

Workers are passing out pamphlets and checking documentation. Tickets in the air waving of those who are staging. Detective Reisen notices a distinguished gentleman who might be Captain of this incredible vessel. Stepping forward prepared for a maritime adventure.

"I am Captain Lockney of the S.S. Marinara. How are ... wow! Appears someone dived in before leaving port."

His sudden disposition is humoring.

"Ready to leave mud, and filth behind, Captain Lockney."

They shake hands.

"Might need hot water to pry those stains out," Captain Lockney jokes.

"In dire need of a good scrubbing and conditioning," Bonnie contends.

"Cool water suits me better."

Laughing together for a few moments.

"Here are the passes for our all-inclusive paid trips."

Captain Lockney scans both tickets into a handheld device. Handing our passes back.

"Here you are! Two passes for a once-in-a-lifetime adventure to Cozumel, Mexico. Enjoy your cruise on the S.S. Marinara!"

A once-in-a-lifetime trip is a bold claim. However, there is no denying an insane amount of detail on the S.S. Marinara. A glossy white base with ridiculous space. Lighting putting off honey-glazed rays.

"I'm excited!" Bonnie shouts.

"Do you dance?" Captain Lockney asks.

"I love dancing! He does as well."

Bonnie latches on to Detective Reisen. Gripping him around the arm—squeezing intensely.

"Wonderful! Tonight, in the club, we have a Halloween-themed dance night. Don't be afraid of the Monster Mash!"

"I can be a monster on the dance floor," Reisen quips.

Laughing together before proceeding forward. Entering inside of a lobby which seems endless. Activities are supplied on each side. A standing post lists directions for rooms, and fun zones. Detective Reisen runs a finger across the directory board stopping where their quarters rest.

"Not too far of a hike."

"We have more than our needed steps today," she says.

"Sorry, dearest. If there was a cart around, I would surely push you."

"You were nearly on my good side until you said that."

They pass bursting sounds, and unique room environments. Showing restraint by not trotting off of the beaten path.

A man walks by blowing his nose nearly in half. A woman dangles on his arm. A purple handkerchief blowing atrociously. Past his red puffy eyes, passengers are bowling. A room they pass feels stuffy.

"I always become seasick," a man groans.

They step away as another man says, "I'll never understand why we drag them along."

The pair is having fun and making progress. Passing a wishing well, water slides, and a fancy restaurant named Rantoul's. Stairs led to more stairs. Ceilings feel as if they could rise higher. Finally reaching their designated room. Hitting the showers with nothing slowing down their pace. No lost time, or lost hours when leisure time is worth a pricey voucher.

Chapter Three: Adrift

In a dark patch of the city—something fierce is smoldering. Two men meet under a viaduct near Lake Michigan. One party attends in a black vehicle. Another party pulls up in a limousine. A window slides down, and a face shows concern.

Black car doors swing open. Out steps a man in a brown overcoat and matching colored hat. An empty alcohol bottle flies out of the limousine window, as he approaches.

"How stressed are you, Jake?"

"That's my second one of those, Greitens," Jake replies.

Eric Greitens reaches into his coat pocket. His hand outstretches, holding a pack of gum, "Take a piece."

Jake Frunk unwraps a piece of gum nervously and begins chewing.

"Take your time," Greitens says.

"Lousy former Mayor Riley dropped the ball. Set us pretty far back on our plans," Jake Frunk relinquishes.

"My office is representing former Mayor Riley in court. You are in the clear," Greitens coaxes.

"How are you so sure?" Jake inquires.

"The prosecution asked for a grand jury against former Mayor Riley. This city is filled with loyalists to the former mayor. City Prosecutor Scotch's case will stall out."

"Scotch has an impressive record," Jake contends.

"I am the best defense attorney in this city, Jake," leaning in closer, "I don't lose in my district," Greitens contends.

Eric Greitens knocks twice on one of the windows.

"You haven't lost yet," Jake says. Slurping off of a bottle. "Make sure Riley doesn't squeal, and I will handle Detective Reisen. His partner as well ... the toolbox, or whatever his name is," Jake Frunk mocks.

"Detective Reisen is on vacation. His partner is no threat to us. Hear me—"

"We tried scaring them, Greitens! Mayor Reinhart will put me out of business if he pieces this together."

"Please, Jake, be rational. You've been drinking. This—"

"Waiting around is the death of every great empire. All my hard work will not go down the drain. Not on my watch!"

"Our hard work, Jake. Be reasonable, think of the opportunity squandered if you're caught making a mistake. Our business is running Chicago the way we see fit. Not murder, not a runaway train, or some moonlight cruise."

"What are you saying, Greitens?"

"Mayor Jake Frunk, that's what the residents of Chicago need," Greitens insists.

"Thank you for the legal advice, Eric Greitens."

Jake faces his chauffeur, "Take me home!"

Eric Greitens shakes his head before leaving. Picking up the flask, Jake Frunk tossed out. Whipping the empty plastic container into Lake Michigan.

In a shadow—out of plain sight—lurks a pair of eyes. A badge in the night surveying a desperate scene outside. Watching every movement with jurisprudence. Being extra careful not to overdo it.

Rising from a power nap hearing the shower curtain slide back. Bonnie jumps out fresher than an Irish spring. Detective Reisen's first thoughts consist of her beauty. Recalling Bonnie's uncanny intuition, blended with an unflappable premonition. Not overthinking, or feeling thoughts sink deeply.

Time for a drink, ready to eat, but craving something sweet. Bonnie presses against him as time cannot tempt them. After absorbing her grace, the shower is a maximum efficient daydreaming space.

Stepping out of the glistening water, and into a snazzy robe.

Bonnie starts growling, "I can't find it!" While digging out her luggage.

"What are you missing?" Detective Reisen probes.

"My Shungite medallion."

"I will aid you in searching."

"Forget it! I am starving, and I hear your stomach talking," Bonnie jibs.

Fresh from head to toe, and out of the door before any clock in the world strikes nine, or four. Down the escalators into a field of pies. Key lime, apple, and many fascinating kinds. Halting in their tracks, before sinking sharp teeth into a slice. Passing decorated venues, on the way toward a full breakfast menu.

A restaurant called, The Last Sauce, catches Detective Reisen's eyes. A giant egg dropping in a pan, lights up above. He moves inside, but not before accidentally rubbing elbows with a slender red-headed woman. Dressed back from the times, when household items were all wooden.

"Out of my way," she growls. Blowing by the couple.

She may have been ghosted, or somebody boosted her ego too high.

"This is the last time!" she shouts.

Out of sight, but still sensing tension slicing wide. Passing by a sign that reads, please, seat yourselves inside. They find a clean cozy table. In less than a minute, a waitress headed toward them. An orange sauce bottle is printed on the corner of her shirt. Not a stain on her neatly pressed purple and orange striped uniform. Is she truly clocked in for work? Maybe their table is her first.

Legs extending far beyond her knees. A full-fledged brunette with hair that's still wet. She sets down menus in front of them.

"My name is Ellen. I will be your waitress this morning. May I start you two out with a beverage?"

"Yes, please. I am dying of thirst," Detective Reisen says.

"Not getting any love?" Ellen asks.

"Excuse you!" Bonnie shouts.

"Two lemonades, please, fast if you will," Detective Reisen interjects. Holding Bonnie back from causing a scene.

"Coming up fast!"

Ellen bolts for the kitchen before breakfast turns vicious. Bonnie starts pursuing Ellen, but I catch her arm. Gently easing her back into the seat. "Be the bigger person, sweetheart." Kissing Bonnie on the cheek, before sitting down.

"I better start eating a lot to become bigger than her."

Chatter fills in the void of The Last Sauce. Each plate is made of blown glass with variously colored designs. A green band displaying stars, and planets around the plate's outer rim. In front of Bonnie lay plates with an orange band incorporating cars, and checkered flags.

"Did you look at the menu, or will you be staying mad?"

"I'm hoping Ellen is smart enough not to return."

"There are plenty of servers around. I'm sure she will swap with one of them."

"Her future may depend on it."

"I hear the food on this cruise line is fantastic," he says.

Drawing attention back to their date, "Look at the menu, please. One dish must be calling your name."

"Nothing is popping out at me."

"Keep looking, beautiful. Something on The Last Sauce's menu will suit you."

"I don't need to keep looking," Bonnie states.

He glances up and meets Bonnie's glowing gaze.

"You suit me perfectly," she says.

Admiration for the opposite sex is too much for any plate to contain. Astonished by one another, their reactions, and motions flow with such ease. If only being a detective was this much of a breeze. Detective Reisen would retire with ease. Living his final days out in peace.

The Last Sauce's theme is covered by a glossy coated green. Baskets and tinsel hang over the eves. Noise breaks free, and the mood is complete peace. Music is playing from a jukebox—a real catchy beat. A few patrons gravitate up to their feet.

On their parade of love, they choose not to rush. This trip is more significant than a hardship of lust. Feelings for Bonnie fuel an ultimate trust. We must set the stage before we move the bus. Not to twist words or mince words. Not to twist her world, but instead, rock her world! Love climaxes where rockets twirl in action.

Bonnie makes worlds shimmer, and darkness quiver. Taking Detective Reisen back to glowing lights at night. When he would hike down by a local river. An insoluble motivation for every case scenario. There has been a lack of decency in humanity recently which worries him ferociously. Let's see if the S.S. Marinara will install hope in Detective Reisen or leave him afloat.

Chapter Four: Power Shift

Guests from all walks of life arrive draped in the finest linen, and latest fashion editions. There is little room left for parking. People nearly trample partygoers while rushing inside.

Jake Frunk is in a purple suit behind a podium. He begins speaking, "Glad everyone made it. Interesting developments are shaking out city-wide. The good news is profit has skyrocketed. Money is not the reason for tonight's get-together. The bad news is, we have too many delinquencies."

The crowd jeers and pumps their fists in anger. People fill in as Jake Frunk wants to catapult from danger. Asserting himself as a true contender, and not a deranged stranger.

"Time to pay up, people!" a man shouts.

Choice words spill out all through the venue.

Jake Frunk motions to quiet the crowd before speaking.

"In days past, I have followed up with elected city officials and relied on them to fix critical issues. I have recently learned from my advisors that this is a bad business practice. Who would have thought being fully compliant is bad for business."

Jake Frunk grins. Raising his arm in the air. Holding a martini with an olive in his left hand. Small chuckles air out an otherwise silent room.

"Under new corrective action, these delinquencies, or defects, as I prefer. Are being corrected as we speak."

Clapping fills the banquet hall stuffed with high-priced antiquities. Jake Frunk takes a swig off of his martini.

"I am a self-made man, who decided to make Chicago home again."

A roar in the banquet hall breaks out as more guests fill in from outside.

"I, Jake Frunk, have been informed by city prosecutor Scotch, and Progressive Task Force 12-Z, that we aren't legitimate."

An outbreak of laughter stirs the crowd.

"They have done all the digging into my taxes they can do. I'm still standing here. We're still standing here!" Jake Frunk shouts.

Slamming his fist down on the podium. All to the crowd's enthusiasm as they egg on famous architect Jake Frunk.

A chant begins, "This is our home! This is our home! This is our home!"

All of this commotion is heard from down the street, and countless blocks over. A delighted Jake Frunk takes a bow.

"I will leave my fellow intellects with a term of endearment. If they come for me, they will surely fall. If they come for us, they will surely fall farther!" Jake Frunk rallies.

A gigantic crowd is enamored, before breaking out into a frenzy. Security guards shield, Jake Frunk, while he exits the facility. A packed house full of newspaper reporters, celebrities, and members of Chicago's top brass instantly pledges their support behind Jake Frunk for Mayor.

In the back of an all-white limousine, Jake Frunk is burning down a cigar. A door opposite Jake Frunk opens. A medium-sized body, with long black hair, and thick legs joins him. She is in a red dress, with matching nails, and lipstick. Black heels slide across the floor mat.

"Great speech."

"Thanks, Mindy," Jake begrudges. Gulping down another shot of liquor, from his private stock.

"Careful with that stuff, Jake. You don't want an ulcer."

"Ha-ha! Always knew you cared," Jake growls.

"Didn't know if you were going to make a Presidential bid out of your diatribe back there," Mindy harps.

"Being President is when you must worry about contracting an ulcer," Jake quips.

Mindy scowls, "Your hospitality is improving. What do you need from me?"

Pouring up another shot, "Gather your best people. Someone is about to have an accident."

"Any other miraculous details?"

Jake slides a file folder across the seat. Mindy opens the maroon folder, and inside lies a picture. A summary is written beneath the target.

"This will cost you ... a fortune, Jake."

"I am prepared to pay accordingly. Make certain an accident occurs. Burn the entire folder when you're finished," Jake Frunk snorts.

"Are you positive this is what you want?" Mindy asks.

"Without a doubt," Jake doubles down.

Mindy continues looking over the file. She doesn't appear enthused, but money is her calling.

"Jake, be a sweetheart for once. Come by tomorrow afternoon."

"What for, Mindy?"

"There is someone I must introduce you to."

"If you want me to meet your hitman, the answer is no."

"Don't be a silly goose. Be a swan and tend to your flock."

"What time should I arrive exactly?"

"Anytime, tomorrow afternoon. Ring for me when you are out front. Gate security will be notified of your arrival."

Mindy runs her fingers along Jake Frunk's arm before exiting his limousine.

Jake Frunk peers forward at his chauffeur, "Head toward Big Clark's Diner."

If there is no time, there is no wait. Problems won't sustain added weight. Weighing fate means counting lesser pain as great. Misconceptions lie in every lesson. Will you take, or give for satisfaction? Temporary actions—meet distractions, and a soundly devised plan is surely gaining traction. Pressure deludes without gainful measures.

Intuitively severed were binds of trust which uncomfortably tethered feelings of mutual respect. Without a satisfaction card left to cut from the deck players went bust. Optioning extremes, and financial engineering schemes. Justice must roll through on a wide beam. A highwire act won't catch a shadow brand of crooks, and thieves.

Smooth Jazz notes play from the surroundings. Listening, lounging, earthly, and grounded. Music and rhythm help meditating minds sing. Piano keys sounded at a soothing outing.

A nest egg is triumphant when found. Grade A eggs are put into a proper omelet. Romance heats up fast but doesn't need to be foiled. Resolutions are a gift, and retribution is amiss. Armour must be worn to avoid being stiffed. Chances are questions and are unfounded if not dug into quickly.

Similarities don't always evolve into parodies. Scarcity could prove to be a smoke screen in the middle of smoke city. Smokestacks which crave a chimney sweep, sit along the city street. An all-white limousine is passing through traffic with ease. Business is best served, and not serviced when stakes are never certain.

Chapter Five: Setting The Table

"Their brochure says—"

"This is the final straw!" a woman screeches. Watch where you are going, you big oaf!"

She shoves a gentleman into a few patiently upstanding patrons. People fall, and a few shouts ring out.

The man who was pushed turns around in disarray. Pointing in her face, "You are way out of line!"

A hush rolls over the establishment. Quieting down conversations as people's heads turn around. Everyone is watching the drama unfolding.

A hand flies in swatting the irate man's finger down, "Get your hand out of my wife's face!" he demands.

"How dare you—"

Before finishing his sentence, the two men are choking each other. They break out into full-on wrestling. Their bodies roll before one is slammed into the lobby.

"Gentleman, please! This is supposed to be a family establishment!" a chef shouts, coming from around the counter.

The woman who initiated the chaos begins attacking the chef with her handbag.

"Where is security when you need them?" Detective Reisen asks.

He makes eye contact with Bonnie before excusing himself from the table.

"This won't take long," he reassures.

"I'm sure that brawl will be wrapped up quickly. I will order for you, sugar. Do you want bacon and eggs?"

"Brunch is in order. Make it a Philly cheese steak with extra grilled onions," Detective Reisen replies.

"Any sides?" Bonnie inquires.

He rushes towards both men who are wrestling in the hallway.

"Coleslaw!" Detective Reisen shouts.

They are grappling and doing a poor job acting. A gray-haired husky man is pitted against a brown-haired buffoon. Both hefty men are unable to gain an advantage. The gray-haired man trips the other fella. They spill onto the floor. When they look up, Detective Reisen stands in the middle of them.

The brown-haired man hastily flips the gray-haired man over. Ready to land a punch with his fist clinched high in the air. Another hand grips his shirt collar.

"Let me teach you—"

Detective Reisen snatches his wrist before he lands a devastating blow.

"Hey! Mind your business!"

"Not a chance," Detective Reisen replies.

"You moron!" he rages.

He releases the elder gray-haired man. Throwing a punch with his opposite hand at Detective Reisen. He ducks underneath and returns fire with a body punch.

Detective Reisen twists his arm in a knot.

"Ugh! Please, no!"

Snapping him over his shoulder, and onto the floor.

"Darn, you, ugh ... ugh," he cries in agony.

Whistles blow as four security personnel members rush forward surrounding Detective Reisen.

One man steps forth, "My name is Roberto, chief of security. I witnessed you striking that brown-haired gentleman. You will need to come with us."

Roberto reaches for Detective Reisen's arm as the other three security personnel move in.

"Wait, just a darn minute!" The older gray-haired man dusts himself off. "That brown-haired screwball picked a fight with me. He couldn't control his obnoxious girlfriend!"

"Slow down old fella we don't need you blowing a gasket," Detective Reisen states.

Two of the security guards tend to the brown-haired man. He is showing symptoms of a concussion. Faintly hearing him writhing in pain on the floor. In my mind, he's giving them a show.

"You sure did a number on that guy. He's still on the ground," Roberto says.

"You're not paying attention, Roberto! That hardwired imbecile was about to finish me off. If it wasn't for this brave soul you are accusing, I would be a dead man!"

Roberto raises an eyebrow, "Is this old fella's story true?"

"Is my story true? My good sir, I have been through a lot of things in life. Never once have I been a liar!" he fumes.

"Yes. The brown-haired man had him pinned down. He wasn't showing any sign of stopping," Reisen explains.

"If both of your stories check out you won't be bothered by us. What are your names, and room numbers in the event we need to speak with you?" Roberto asks.

A pen, and notepad at his disposal.

"Someone picks up that no good dirty slouch. People need room to walk through here," the gray-haired man jokes.

Two security members assist helping the brown-haired man up to his feet, but he plummets back down. Another security guard is radioing for medical staff.

"Detective Reisen, Room number three hundred six."

"Detective ... Detective! Oh, hey, pal! Sorry about this whole ordeal. You may take your leave," Roberto states.

"If I will be of more assistance, look me up."

"Yes, sir! Detective, sir! Shouldn't be any issue at all, sir!"

"Farewell for now," Detective Reisen chuckles.

A security member taps Roberto's shoulder, whispering something. He hurriedly tucks his notepad away.

"Your help is appreciated, old timer," Reisen commends.

"Not a problem. Thank you for punching in!"

Two members of Roberto's security detail are on each end of a stretcher, carrying the brown-haired man away. Two nurses on each side work on him. They move toward the medical bay. The slender bully of a woman has vanished. These events sent many people into a panic.

Peering around unable to spot which direction the gray-haired man wandered off in. A truly puzzling moment that expanded hunger. Heading back towards Bonnie. Before taking another step, someone is tugging on his arm.

"Quite a punch you are packing," Captain Lockney says.

Nearly unable to form words in disbelief.

"Helps me out of trouble, more than not."

Captain Lockney drops his arm before they parlay.

"Glad that elderly gray-haired man spoke up for you. If he didn't, I would have."

"Thank you for sticking around."

"You put on a good show. I have seen that gray-haired fella around before. He is a kooky one."

"He's different, in not so many words," Reisen confers.

"That's a polite way of describing him. We hold a charity boxing event for the Thirty-Forty Organization. Unfortunately, my fighter is sick. Are you interested in taking his place?"

"What's in it for me?" Detective Reisen probes.

"The winner will have their entire trip's package reimbursed. Plus, two passes for a free flight anywhere around the world!"

"Where do I sign up?" Detective Reisen inquires.

"Eagerness is the trait of a strong man!" Captain Lockney shakes his hand, "Meet me down below sea level, at five o'clock pm sharp. You won't miss any of the signs!" Captain Lockney hollers, as he walks off.

Rotating back towards Bonnie, and brunch. A slight touch of swagger adds bounce to each step. Arriving at last with their orders on track.

"Sorry for the wait," he apologizes.

A substitute server dishes out sides.

"Perfectly fine, honey," Bonnie replies.

"Hello, sir. My name is, Jerod. What is your choice of beverage?"

"Fresh orange juice would be nice," Reisen replies.

Jerod darts away from us. Bonnie chews on ice cubes.

"Wasn't he much more professional?" Bonnie asks.

"How could anyone not love good service?" Reisen asks.

"He may be a tad bit underwhelming," Bonnie says.

"He was refreshing, but your observation is heartfelt."

"Thank you," she replies, stabbing her food.

"Do I dare ask, how you managed the server swap?"

"Ellen, caught my drift. Will you?"

"Completely."

"We have a four-day cruise ahead of us," Bonnies says.

"That is what we paid for."

Bonnie smiles while looking up at me, "Our first day should be spent apart."

"Already ... I thought we were off to a hot start."

"We're sharing a room, dork."

"We're sharing more than that," Detective Reisen says.

Sliding her drink over and taking a sip. Bonnie fans me with napkins. "You are terrible at this."

"I am still an excellent listener."

"Then I should only need to explain one time. We each need to find an exciting activity for the other partner to do."

"If you want to spend a lot of money, and not see my eyes widen, say that sweetheart."

"You know better. I love splurging on myself."

"Seems my charm has worn off," Reisen confesses.

Sipping her drink, "What do you mean?"

"Over in the hallway, I performed a heroic feat. When I return, my lovely fiancée is requiring space."

Poking her food with a fork, "You're terrible with dramatics. The rocking of the boat must have watered you down."

Leaning around the table—kissing Bonnie on the lips.

"You notice my greatest qualities."

"You respect my personal choices."

"If you want to be apart for today, fine by me. Shall we begin eating?"

"Sweet! I am finished!" Bonnie shouts.

"You hardly—"

Bonnie clasps Detective Reisen's face, kissing him deeply before whisking away into the crowd.

Jerod returns with freshly squeezed orange juice.

"Hello, sir. Before I take my break is there anything else I can grab for you?"

"Did you say you're going on break?"

"That's right, sir. I have an hour break for lunch."

"Do you want to hear a story?"

"Why not?"

"Please, grab a seat, Jerod. It is good to meet you. Here goes a noble story I believe you will enjoy ...."

Chapter Six: An Orange Zone

Shopping is a select choice on an all-inclusive paid cruise. Depending on who you are with—impulse purchasing is highly unavoidable. Not only does Bonnie utilize choice words, but she also solidifies choice decisions. A fitting touch in a world flush with a daily rush. I don't know if the Windy Wind-Up newspaper misses Bonnie, more than she misses her column. Certain issues won't be pressed, certain information Bonnie doesn't disclose. Better Detective Reisen sticks with the latter in uncharted matters.

Heels click while streaming lights blink. Bonnie arrives at a bookstore, her traveling wardrobe is elite. An orange sign in the window is designed as a library. In big bold letters bolster the word, open.

"Welcome to The Fellow Flamingo! We have a jubilee of groovy books on our shelves," says a woman rocking bronzed hair. An orange flower is tucked above her left ear.

A lone customer is checking out a book. Bonnie browses around before the other woman sees herself out.

"Thank you for asking, dear. I love the orange flower for a nice touch. Startling bright colors, and they complete your outfit. You know how to dress," Bonnie admonishes.

"You're a doll! Where is the lucky man?"

"Soon to be lucky! He's on the cruise. I don't need him attached at the hip yet," Bonnie jokes.

"You slay me! I'm Celina. An absolute pleasure to make your acquaintance."

"I'm Bonnie and thank you for having a bookstore on board. The Fellow Flamingo is the only bookstore on board!"

"Girl don't get me started! Some cruises I wish, I just wish I had more competition going on. Then I remember that being the only sheriff in town is sort of a good thing, honey."

"Especially in this economy," Bonnie reaffirms.

"Amen! I know that's all truth being spoken in here!"

"Until you need backup."

Celina bursts out laughing, "Ow! There you go again! She's bad! She's a bad lady up in The Fellow Flamingo!"

"Did anyone ever tell you, you're hilarious?" Bonnie asks.

"They tell me all types of things, but I'm done listening."

"I'm right there with you," Bonnie replies.

"We picked up a truckload of new books after we docked at the last port. Any mystery you may be looking for?"

"How about a book with an orange cover to match your orange flower," Bonnie requests.

"A classy move!" Celina hollers.

Celina checks the database of The Fellow Flamingo on a company computer.

"You won't believe it! How about, 'The Orange Rock' by Rock F. Dewgel."

"Sold! Take my money, and then I'm heading for a drink," Bonnie discloses.

"It is happy hour at the Tiki Bar. If you don't mind, I will guide you there?"

"Lead the way, Celina. Always happy to make a great friend."

"Thank you. A bunch of stiffs aboard lately. Times are changing people. Making folks cold to a loving world."

"Amen to that! Shall we change the times for the better?"

Celina's face is flush with enthusiasm. She gives Bonnie a high-five as both ladies are strolling outside. Celina reaches back flipping the open sign to closed.

Back in the windy city of Chicago, past weeping willows—down around Lake Shore Drive. Tides slide, and tensions clip overdrive as two figureheads begin coming alive.

A dining room sits dimly lit. Two shadows arise from the dense mist. Each man sits at a booth opposed to the window. A city's future in limbo. Progressive Task Force 12-Z is in dire need of funding. When monsters take the form of men, bold officers are entrusted to serve them a slice of justice.

"What is the itinerary behind Mayor Reinhart's competition?" Captain Davis inquires. Rubbing a hand warmer together.

"The heat is on in this joint. Are you cold?" Dewalt asks.

"Had a chill all morning," Captain Davis replies.

"If you're becoming sick, don't start touching stuff."

A waitress slides into the picture, "My name is Suclese. I will be your server today."

She drops two menus and sets down two glasses of water. Placing straws on top of the table.

Detective Dewalt unwraps a straw and sticks it in a cup of water. He takes a long sip. He holds the menu up.

Captain Davis doesn't blink while warming his hands up.

"Please, give me a ... moment," he sneezes.

"I'll give you gentlemen some time," Suclese replies.

She checks on another table of hungry patrons.

"Is your favorite appetizer on the menu?"

"Maybe."

"Break the news, Dewalt!" Captain Davis shouts.

Detective Dewalt intently studies Big Clark's menu.

"The foundation is being built," Detective Dewalt states.

"I didn't know you started doing construction. Congratulations! I thought you were out doing real detective work. Instead, you're laying bricks down."

Detective Dewalt burst out laughing.

"You cannot stay calm. That is why you're in a captain's uniform."

"Are you the great detective worried about my job description, or my temperament?" Captain Davis probes.

"I am concerned about your tail," Detective Dewalt says.

"My tail! How many times must I save your rear end?"

"I figure, we will see how many lives a cat truly has."

Suclese reenters the picture pouring Captain Davis a cup of coffee. Passing Detective Dewalt an orange juice, rendering him stunned.

Captain Davis's face runs long with amazement, "This is magic in a cup! Thank you!"

"You're welcome. One of the ladies in the kitchen tipped me off on to how you take your coffee," Suclese unveils.

"A nifty use of your resources. Impressive, and delicious," Detective Dewalt proclaims.

"You're good at what you do. Have you ever thought of becoming a police officer?" Captain Davis inquires.

"Don't get the poor girl killed. Let her enjoy the fruits of her years," Detective Dewalt protests.

"Stop confusing her," Captain Davis rebuttals.

"Believe it or not, I contemplated becoming a police officer for quite a few years. Never knew how to start, or where to begin. Had to pay bills, and here I am," Suclese relinquishes.

A shady character wearing a ski mask rushes into the restaurant. Gripping a snub-nosed revolver. A medium-sized bag wrapped around his shoulder.

"Everyone put your hands on the table!" Smashing in the cashier's nose, "Empty the register in the bag!"

His revolver is aimed at the cashier's face, "Don't bleed all over the money."

The cashier fills the bag quickly, trying not to stain any dollar bills.

"Unload the safe while I make my rounds. People, set your valuables on the table!" he shouts.

The cashier finishes loading the bag. People are frantically placing their valuables at the edge of their tables.

"Drop your weapon!" Captain Davis shouts.

Detective Dewalt slides out of the booth on one knee. Their weapons are drawn on the bandit. He's directly lined up in their sights.

The masked bandit turns to shoot but is knocked unconscious. Flopping down on the floor, after being dinged from behind.

Suclese stands over top of the bandit clutching a metal pan, "This will be the only time someone's food goes cold on my shift."

Detective Dewalt and Captain Davis rush in handcuffing the robber with no resistance. Additional police officers quickly swarm the scene and take the suspect into custody.

"You're hired, Suclese!" Captain Davis shouts.

"What in heaven's name do you mean?" Dewalt inquires.

Suclese lets out a high-pitched shriek. Patrons inside Big Clark's Diner shield their ears. Nothing refrains anyone from clapping gently, after witnessing Suclese's heroism.

"Thank you dearly for this opportunity!"

Suclese hugs Captain Davis before sprinting back into the kitchen. Unable to conceal her enthusiasm over the latest exciting news on what otherwise was an average day.

"In all honesty, Captain Davis, I have to speak up. Are you sure about bringing on a rookie during a time such as this?"

"I'm banking on it," Captain Davis reassures.

Detective Dewalt shows a grave look of uncertainty.

"We will make arrangements after we eat breakfast," Captain Davis decides.

After discussing the attempted robbery with a handful of responding officers, Detective Dewalt rejoins Captain Davis.

Chapter Seven: Memorable Moments

"Always count on the unexpected around here."

"Talent is recognizable when you have been around Chicago long enough," Captain Davis states.

Dewalt rolls his eyes, "You are long in the tooth."

Captain Davis grins before taking a sip of coffee.

"Who do you think found you, greenhorn?"

"No complaints, only compliments, Captain Davis."

Detective Dewalt raises a sweet glass of orange juice, with no pulp, and has a big gulp.

"What's the crack-pot architect plotting?" Davis inquires.

"Jake Frunk is working on becoming Mayor of Chicago."

Captain Davis nearly spits out coffee. Wiping his mouth free of residue with a napkin.

"The loose cannon architect wants to reign as king of the castle he helped designed."

"Jake Frunk is expanding on a blueprint," Detective Dewalt continues.

"Do you mean, Jake Frunk's blueprint?"

"Not quite sure, it's still a gray area," Detective Dewalt says.

"Don't give me a handful of joker cards. The only gray area is outside up in fluffy clouds," Captain Davis growls.

"Be helpful if a few of those clouds cleared."

"Clever metaphors never make me feel wholesome," Captain Davis rebuffs.

"Jake Frunk held a private fundraiser last night. Big names, large money, and a huge reaction. Massive financial donors are pledging their support behind him. He's a late-entry candidate, but he is an undeniable deadly force."

"You are full of jokes today. Your assignment was to figure out what Mayor Reinhart is up against. Including, what we might be facing during election season. Is this the best story you can conjure up?" Captain Davis probes.

A television in the diner rolls footage of Jake Frunk shaking hands with supporters at a fundraiser from last night. Captain Davis and Detective Dewalt view the live broadcast.

"All factual information is rolling in, Captain. Jake Frunk went up on stage and belted out a hypercritical speech. We don't know what this issue spells for Chicago yet," Dewalt details.

"Jake Frunk being elected mayor spells anarchy."

"Provides, Suclese an opportunity for field training."

"Didn't take you long to come around, Detective Dewalt. Jake Frunk's motivations are unnerving each of us."

Old Man Winter heaves a surprise storm upon the windy city of Chicago. Snowflakes come crashing down, while strong winds pile snow into mounds. Salt trucks begin full deployment. Roaming city streets, where yellow lights atop trucks pulsate. Snowplow drivers are out in full force, with full tumblers beside them. Unilateral rumblings deep underground of Chicago's busy bustling streets.

Captain Davis and Detective Dewalt are sensing signs of trouble.

"We haven't flinched," Detective Dewalt reassesses.

"We're entering a danger zone. Do you understand?" Captain Davis probes.

"Yes, I do. We have no other choice."

"We have another choice," Captain Davis contends.

"What is our plan b?"

"We resign," Captain Davis suggests.

"Your acting still needs some gloss, but your material is punchy."

Detective Dewalt, pats Captain Davis on the back. Finishing off his glass of orange juice.

"If you keep slugging down that orange juice, you will be in the orange zone," Captain Davis warns.

"Much better than the gray zone," Dewalt admits.

"Thank you for noticing a true stroke of genius while being brushed," Captain Davis says, tipping his cap.

A loud beeping sound turns both men cold.

"Whoa! Wait! No, no, no!" Captain Davis shouts.

Rushing outside all too late. His cries are to no avail. A public works truck backs into his police cruiser.

"Why, me!" Captain Davis howls.

Detective Dewalt leans on his car roaring with laughter.

"This never happens when Detective Reisen, and I eat here."

A tow truck spurts—as Chicago's underbelly churns. Waves skim against the S.S. Marinara. Amber-colored skies light a promising path. Multiple talents keep a party alive. Feels as if they are moving with a riptide. Propellers spinning, and endless headwinds riffing. Excessive paraffin, which could invoke uncontrollable flames. More than enough to set them ablaze. A romance on fire abstaining from falling lame.

Bonnie Butterfield, and Celina sit on two stools at a Tiki Bar. Passing time aboard the S.S. Marinara.

"Two Long Island iced teas!" Celina hollers at the barkeep. Piercing through a crowd's loud resonating ambiance.

"Two long islands coming at you!" he shouts.

Quickly making two Long Island iced teas. Setting each beverage in front of Bonnie, and Celina.

"Thank you, Jasper," Celina says.

"No worries, Celina. Who is your friend?"

"Oh, hello! My name is—"

"Her name is taken, Jasper. Assist your other patrons!"

"I only—"

"We're all good here, mister man," Celina interrupts.

"Sorry ladies, but I have a job to do. A real nice pleasure meeting you, taken," Jasper winks, before hustling over to a thirsty patron.

"Let's sit somewhere more secluded," Celina suggests.

Both women scoot into a pair of chairs. A serene ocean view awaits them from their elevated positions.

"A real cruise is when my feet are up, and I'm being fanned," Celina remarks, sipping her Long Island iced tea.

"Make it two fans," Bonnie replies.

"You catch my drift. I wish the S.S. Marinara would do more for us. Great place to work, but awful floors to work on."

"Floors and fans were the last two things Platinum Cruise Lines worried about," Bonnie concurs.

"I knew you were the right person to have a drink with."

"What gave me away?" Bonnie probes.

"Your sense of humor. People are rushing into bad situations, and forgoing simple aspects of life," Celina rants.

Bonnie sits back in her chair, sipping through a straw.

"Wherever your line of thinking is heading, count me in."

"You deep dive into being a friend, instead of frenemies."

"What a vivid way of describing me."

Bonnie proposes a toast, "Celina, here's to our sleek, and dynamic friendship. Whether on land or out at sea."

Bonnie raises her glass as does Celina. Clinking their beverages together, "Cheers!" they shout.

Slowly sipping away, Bonnie scowls heavily over Celina's shoulder. "Is there a ghost behind me?"

"Ha-ha! No, dear. A woman caused a stir at The Last Sauce earlier. She might start up again," Bonnie explains.

Bonnie sips her drink slowly, locked in on the slender woman. Styling a black hat, with her red hair showing on all sides. An orange cheetah print ascot tucked atop her bright white pantsuit.

Celina mirrors her head using Bonnie's example, "Should we find a better vantage point?"

"Let's boogie," Bonnie replies.

Both women scurry off for a better look.

"Wait!" Celina hollers.

"What? Oh, right. Our drinks!" Bonnie relays.

Both women rush back shouting, "Our drinks! Our drinks!"

Almost knocking the table over while picking up their beverages.

"Hurry up and slam it! Tiki Bar alcohol is decent, but the good stuff is in my fridge," Celina says.

Peeling off around the corner, almost tripping themselves. A toxic scene is unfolding in front of them.

"What is happening?" Celina asks.

"Hold on," Bonnie whispers, "I am trying to listen."

A thin-lipped woman argues with a dapper gentleman. Heehawing at a snobbish snaggletooth vixen.

"You are psychotic!" he shouts.

"My drink is empty, and money is running low. Patience for your pin-headed egotistic attitude is finally gone!"

"Beatrice, knock it off. You are causing a scene!"

"Hubert, you are on my last nerve. I am leaving!" Splashing the remains of her drink in his face. Tripping Hubert down to the ground. His glasses fly off, and she is gone.

"Oh, no, she didn't!" Celina shouts.

"She did, and it was messy," Bonnie responds.

Hubert is dripping soaking wet. Using his sleeves, and undershirt to dry himself off.

"Wait a minute ... I know him!" Bonnie shouts. She runs to the Tiki Bar counter and grabs a stack of napkins.

"Who is he?" Celina asks, bewildered.

Bonnie darts past Celina in a trance.

"My boss from the newspaper, Hubert!" Bonnie screeches.

She is racing toward Hubert with napkins ready for use.

Chapter Eight: A Delight And A Fright

Detective Reisen finishes his meal and conversation with Jerod. Where he shared the story, Three Down by Preston Olson with him. Captain Lockney retakes the ship's wheel. Detective Dewalt and Captain Davis face down the barrel of riding together. Eliminating the quiet, and comforts of solo patrolling. Detective Reisen wades through a crowd of hungry patrons. He is forging a separate path. Bonnie, and Celina deal with a fiasco's aftermath.

In the direction Captain Lockney is tasked, is where Detective Reisen fast tracks. Down the escalators, through an elevator, and sliding around stairs occupied by stargazers. Captain Lockney wasn't lying about the signs. Noises bellow from inside. Pushing in a metal bar on double doors and they open wide.

A tall muscle-bound man bounces around the boxing ring. Lean, rugged, and chiseled to his core. A few men shadowbox the air, unbothered by my entrance. A sparring partner is in the ring being pushed against the ropes with a vengeance. Another man sits on a bench, possibly his coach.

Heavy doors close behind me as steps immediately proceed. A man with a silly black hat enters.

"We have been waiting for Captain Lockney's fighter," he says, in a heavily marinated French accent.

Standing unafraid, "I am a fighter. Where is Captain Lockney?" Detective Reisen probes.

"Steering the ship," he jokes.

"You must be the comedic talent onboard," Reisen quips.

Extending his hand for me to shake, "They call me Exhausting Eugene."

Shaking hands with a firm grip before leaning in, "I am, Detective Reisen."

"Glad to meet you, champ. Do you truly want to fight, Owana?" Eugene asks, pointing to the ring.

Fixing their focus as Owana finishes warming up in his corner. The bell rings, and Owana starches his opponent. His sparring partner flies out of the ring. A few men training on exercise equipment assist the fallen boxer.

Owana slides out of the boxing ring.

His cornerman tosses him a towel, "Great work, Owana! Fantastic work! Let's change your wraps in the back, and prepare for tonight's big fight," a man says.

"Who is he?" Detective Reisen probes.

"Pinchard. He is, Owana's trainer," Eugene explains.

Owana pats the towel around his face collecting any sweat. Before reaching the hangar's end he pauses. Glaring at Detective Reisen—with an evil eye. A thin smirk rises on his face before fading out of sight.

"Please, show me to the changing room," Reisen says.

"Follow me," Exhausting Eugene responds.

Our trek continues into an annex outside of the initial boxing ring's radius. Chilly air blowing across their faces. Workbenches are set up in a far south-east corner. Formed into a wrapping, and supply station. A few chairs lay scattered around where people may sit. One fridge stands in a corner straight ahead. A speed bag is installed near a wall. Lighting is poorly lit around a big black punching bag where shadows exist. Exhausting Eugene swings at the speed bag in passing.

"Is this the dungeon they bring Owana's victims before a great giant slaughter?" Detective Reisen inquires.

"Hey, ... you're pretty funny. Save your enthusiasm for Owana," Eugene retorts.

"Air is pretty thin in here," Detective Reisen suggests.

"Usually how Owana finishes his victims off. Cutting off their air supply," Exhausting Eugene mocks.

"Open mic starts right before the fight. Don't be tardy."

"Low oxygen has occurred for eons below deck," he says.

Detective Reisen shakes off his heavier clothing. Moving toward the punching bag.

"Let me put your wrist wraps on. You may warm up all you want afterward. No need to risk an injury."

Exhausting Eugene cuts and prepares the wraps at a small station. "Once the wraps are snug. We will see if they need adjusting."

"Hold the punching bag," Detective Reisen demands.

"What's wrong? Hey, detective, I didn't mean to upset—"

"Get over here. Hold that punching bag, as if there is food inside," Detective Reisen interrupts.

Exhausting Eugene wraps his arms around the punching bag, "What are you doing?"

Detective Reisen paws at the punching bag with a left hand. Following up with a stiff jab from the same hand. A third punch flies in. A counter-right hook pushes Eugene back. Detective Reisen repeats the sequence of punches. Knocking Eugene farther back until he slips off.

"You will be, Owana's toughest challenger by far," he claims.

Detective Reisen studies the bag before moving back toward a short table, "Does Owana have a weakness?"

"Wishful thinking asking me that, son. You know what they say?"

"What do they say?" Detective Reisen asks.

"A closed mouth won't get fed."

"Should I talk during the fight?"

"Save your breath."

"Truthfully, what I tell every fighter who's been down here is work your punches to the body. Keep your head off the center line. You might survive until the final bell."

Stretching my arms out on the table. Exhausting Eugene begins wrapping my wrists, and knuckles. Knocking the first wrap out effortlessly.

"Your other arm, please," Eugene says.

Positioning my arm closer. Eugene fixes white tape around snugly, "How does that feel?"

"Wonderful," Detective Reisen says.

Eugene grins while nodding his head, "Right on. Let's make certain each glove fits."

Eugene searches for a pair of boxing gloves. He returns with a pair still wrapped in plastic. Green with black trim, and a golden snake decal on top.

"Tonight, you have to fight like the viper my friend."

"Let's hope my sting is vicious enough for Owana."

Exhausting Eugene makes certain my gloves are properly fastened.

"The punching bag is all yours," he says.

Fanning out his arms wide, before digging into his coat pocket. Pulling out a cigar case, "Do you mind if I light up in here?"

Stepping toward the daunting black punching bag. The letter, p, is imprinted on it. Simple jabs, one-two punch combos, which build into power shots.

"Doesn't bother me."

"Nice, and nicer," Exhausting Eugene says.

Detective Reisen is grunting while channeling his breathing. Ripping the punching bag with a left hook, side stepping, with sizzling footwork. Landing three punch combinations. Rinsing, and repeating his actions. Focused, and homing in on the task at hand. Boxing the giant Owana.

"You may have a chance against Owana after all," Exhausting Eugene coaxes.

He steps aside from the punching bag.

"Don't butter me up," Detective Reisen jokes.

"You are right. Anyway, there are a lot of people who buy a ticket for the raffle behind this operation. All in the name of a charitable cause. You are doing them a huge favor."

"How did you figure that out?" Detective Reisen probes.

"Not many people want to fight, Owana."

"If you don't imagine your problems as big, they won't wear for worse," Detective Reisen states.

"Ha-ha. With all due respect detective, you are a wild card. Even more surprising you accepted a challenge after being notified."

"What was I notified of?"

"How, Owana broke the last fella's neck," Eugene reveals, before patting me on the shoulder.

Feeling betrayed—Captain Lockney didn't inform me prior.

Throwing a towel over his shoulder, "Let's take our show on the road!" Exhausting Eugene shouts.

A towel Exhausting Eugene must throw in if I am made a fool of during the featured bout. Walking out of the door heading toward the boxing ring. Reaching the ropes full of hope. Looking up as Owana is in the ring, staring my way.

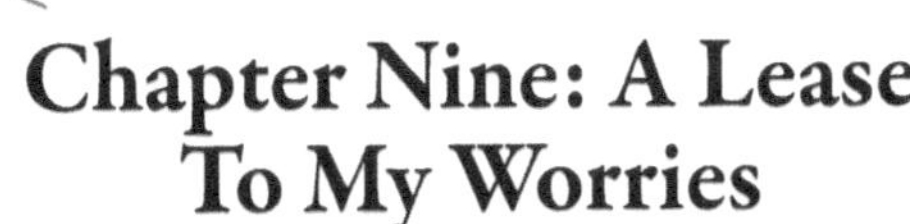

Chapter Nine: A Lease
To My Worries

"Silly, cop had his car double parked. Garbage truck turned it into trash," Jake Frunk mocks.

A deep voice muffles, "His cruiser will be in the scrapyard by nightfall."

"At least they apprehended the robber before I did," Jake Frunk jokes.

"An honorary amateur for attempting a heist on a dive restaurant amid rush hour," the odd man says.

"Without street knowledge, or manners, you could end up a terrible crook," Jake Frunk states.

Jake Frunk slothfully eats a prestigious plated breakfast. Bronzed hash browns, premium sausage, and cheesy eggs.

"Police love filing paperwork. Pork Chop will pencil-push his way to a chief of police role in no time. He looks familiar," Jake Frunk elaborates.

A blonde-haired, blue-eyed, long-faced thug is dining across from Jake Frunk, examining both officers of the peace in question.

"If one of them becomes chief of police, we will cash in on easy street," he says.

Both men instinctively exhaust laughter. Jake Frunk taps pepper on his eggs. The odd man crunches food faster.

"Troy, you were recommended to me by a very noble associate of mine. My question for you is simple. Is this assignment a fit for a man of your gallant valor?"

Jake Frunk finishes eating. His plate is clean, and his eyes are radiating. Glancing up—hinging on a response he desperately wants.

Troy digs into more food, "I will have your fish fried."

"Job yields a quarter of a million dollars. Your payment and vehicle are waiting in lot number six along Madison Avenue. Drop the car off at the airport, and board your plane."

"Where do I head towards after I land in Mexico?" Troy asks.

"After you land, walk outside, and a green car will be your wheels."

"How do I identify the green car if there is more than one?"

"A cherry red air freshener hanging from the rear-view mirror. You won't miss it," Jake Frunk reinforces.

"Where do I travel afterward?"

"There is a map in the car. Your destination is marked."

"Isn't this a bit of a scavenger hunt?" Troy asks.

"Safer to do business this way," Jake Frunk coaxes.

"I'm still listening," Troy says.

"A boat will be prepared for you. Security will be expecting you at the guard shack. They will open the gate, and you will drive down to board the speedboat."

"How do I make my way onto the cruise ship?"

"Plans on how to lose the boat are onboard. The cruise liner will stop for fuel and sightseeing. Crewmen will conduct safety checks. People will be taking pictures ... avoid them."

"A lot of hoops to jump through," Troy worries.

"There is a lot of money and special interest at stake," Jake Frunk counters.

"Fair enough. Do I jump on board at a refueling station?"

"Correct," Jake Frunk confirms.

"Thank you for the opportunity, I accept," Troy says. Outstretching his hand, Jake Frunk shakes in agreement.

Along the S.S. Marinara excitement is wading in waves of contamination.

"Oh, my, goodness gracious!" Bonnie shouts. Drying Hubert's face off perfidiously.

"How dare that wretch try drowning you!" Celina roars.

"Thank you, ladies, one thousand times," Hubert says.

Hubert is a tall lanky man with grayish-brown hair and a feathered mustache. Light facial hair in a blue suit, with a black undershirt. Sporting a fancy timepiece, and a diamond band. A blue bow tie with black silk down to his blue dress shoes.

"You are dressed way too nice to be drenched," Celina bellows.

Celina assists in wiping all of the liquids free from Hubert's face.

"Thank you. Seriously, thank you," Hubert replies. "You are always on top of the story, aren't you, Bonnie," he laughs.

"Ha-ha! I am surprised to see you here. Didn't think, Hubert Hattendoff did cruises," Bonnie confesses.

"Due to my supposed fiancé, I'm here," Hubert admits.

"And drenched," Celina adds.

"Sadly, yes. Before I was able to take a dip in the pool," Hubert decries.

"Sorry about your experience, Hubert. This is my new friend, Celina," Bonnie introduces.

"Pleasure to meet your acquaintance, Celina. Any friend of Bonnie's is a welcome sight," Hubert expresses.

"Awe, thank you. You are a charmer, Hubert. Do you need me to have a chat with your fiancée?" Celina asks.

"Please, no. That won't be necessary," Hubert coughs.

"Say, ... would you two marvelous professionals accompany me to the boxing event tonight?" Hubert inquiries.

"A boxing match ... here on the ship?" Bonnie inquires.

"Oh, yes! For charity of course," Hubert rallies.

"We love entertainment!" Celina shouts.

"And charity!" Bonnie energizes.

Rain douses rock-hard pavement. Dark clouds converge encouraging severe weather. Weird occurrences strengthening currents where oceans fill canals, and rivers. A remittance of courage outlines haunting clues with impertinence. Deciding factors tussle over a greater purpose.

"I am receiving a call," Captain Davis says.

"Quick, jump in my car," Detective Dewalt replies.

A tow truck scampers away, with Captain Davis's vehicle. Detective Dewalt hustles to unlock his car door. Permitting, Captain Davis inside from ongoing brutal conditions.

Captain Davis answers his cell phone, "Hello, Mayor Reinhart ..."

Captain Davis is puzzled as the phone call quickly ends. Tucking his cell phone into his coat pocket.

"What is wrong?" Detective Dewalt probes.

"Mayor Reinhart wants to see us. Says, the matter is imminent. Head for Chicago City Hall, Detective Dewalt."

Detective Dewalt focuses on pulling out from his parking spot on the curb.

"Must be a big assignment if Mayor Reinhart wouldn't fully say what's happening," Detective Dewalt insinuates.

"Let's pray, Mayor Reinhart isn't handing out pink slips," Captain Davis says.

Detective Dewalt peers over at Captain Davis, before driving off. Glass shatters all around them, as bullets are dumped into the car.

"Ambush!" Detective Dewalt shouts.

Captain Davis undoes his seat belt and out comes his sidepiece. Firing back through the shattered window. Detective Dewalt flings his door open and cocks back his pistol. Dashing around the police cruiser emptying his clip.

The gunman lies dead in a pool of blood. Rain washes his bodily fluids into a drainage system nearby.

Detective Dewalt rushes back to the passenger side where Captain Davis is sitting, "Captain Davis! Are you okay?"

"I am fine. Call this into dispatch," Captain Davis states.

Reaching for the radio, while rain blasts Captain Davis in his face. Snot trickling from his nose. Both of their hearts are pumping full of anxiety while one heart ceases to beat any longer.

Detective Dewalt hugs Captain Davis, as he slides out of the car.

"Lunatic, should have waited until after the rain."

"Why is that?" Detective Dewalt probes.

"He would've had a clear shot."

They start laughing as Detective Dewalt gives Captain Davis a friendly shove. Wiping a tear, or two from their eyes. Tires screech loudly as a car flies out from the alley. Detective Dewalt initiates a pursuit.

Captain Davis grabs Detective Dewalt by his arm, "You will only wind-up dead," he warns.

Captain Davis eases off of his arm.

Detective Dewalt straightens his windbreaker out.

"Please, help me cover the window. There is a tarp in the trunk," Detective Dewalt says.

Captain Davis steps toward the trunk as Detective Dewalt unlocks it. They fasten the tarp inside using string, and some tape from the glove compartment. A temporary covering which will protect the interior from water damage.

"There is a hand sweeper and a towel in the trunk. Brush the glass off of your seat. Lay the towel down after."

"Thanks for protecting my behind," Captain Davis jokes.

"That is as close as I am willing to come near it."

Both men chuckle while an ambulance and responding units arrive.

"We will hear what Mayor Reinhart has to say. Afterward, we shall change vehicles," Captain Davis states.

Detective Reisen is warming up with Owana. They bounce around the boxing ring. Not feeling his power until a right hook connects with Detective Reisen's shoulder. Mixing in a few feints, as Detective Reisen leads with his left foot. Ripping into Owana's body with two heavy blows. He straightens up when Detective Reisen pops him with a left uppercut. Dazing Owana, making him cover up. Wanting to do damage, but he is being overwhelmed. A barrage of punches backs Owana up into the ropes. His financial backers begin losing hope.

Owana is wildly winging punches as Detective Reisen is only seeing red. Owana lands a few solid punches. Even staggering Detective Reisen momentarily, but the damage is done. Owana starts circling away, fatigued, and winded. The crowd is losing their minds when Detective Reisen cuts off, Owana's lead leg. Landing a right hook and smashing, Owana's jawline. Dropping, Owana to the canvas.

Captain Lockney assumes the role of official referee, and steps in. He begins counting to ten.

"You don't have to keep going. There is nothing to prove," Detective Reisen pleads.

Owana spits out blood, "Are you scared to fight?"

"Not scared at all. Worried you might not understand the lesson I came to teach," Detective Reisen explains.

"Then quit running your mouth, and let's see some fighting!" Pinchard howls.

Spectators around both fighters shout, "On with it!"

Both boxers are fighting pound for pound, and blow for blow. People react as if they have never seen a fight before.

Chapter Ten: Double Investigation

Detective Dewalt and Captain Davis arrive at Chicago City Hall. Stepping out of the damaged vehicle during midday. Pressing up each step and shuffling through the main lobby. Both men reach Mayor Reinhart's office and begin contemplating their options.

Greeted by Mayor Reinhart's Secretary, "Hey, you two! Mayor Reinhart is expecting each of you."

"Always happy to see the mayor," Captain Davis replies.

"What about me?" Katrina asks.

"Katrina, you brighten up my day," Captain Davis states.

Detective Dewalt tries his best not to laugh.

Katrina's face turns blush, "Oh, my ... my day may have just started, but now my day is going places."

Katrina presses a button as buzzing sounds echo abroad. A long metal latch on the door unlocks.

"Mayor Reinhart will see you now," Katrina states.

Each man tips their cap toward Katrina. Captain Davis pushes ahead as Detective Dewalt accompanies him.

"There you are gentleman!" Pointing at them, before facing his dartboard.

A swift thud rings out across the room.

"Glad to see you both in one piece," Mayor Reinhart says.

"Bullseye!" Mayor Reinhart shouts.

"Well done," Captain Davis says.

"Excellent placement," Detective Dewalt concurs.

"Thank you, men. Recently, darts caught my interest again. An old tricky habit that made me a lot of dough back in the day," Mayor Reinhart elaborates.

They all laugh as Mayor Reinhart wheels out a discreet liquor cabinet. Silk burgundy drapes reach down past a pair of windowsills. One bookcase in each of the corners facing Captain Davis, and Detective Dewalt. Mayor Reinhart closes the blinds on each window.

"The bad weather is clearing up outside. Help yourselves and have a drink."

"We would love to join you for a drink, Mayor Reinhart, but we are on duty," Captain Davis replies.

"No, you're not!" Mayor Reinhart shouts. "As of this very minute, you two fine officers are off of the clock."

"Do you mean we're relieved of duty, sir?" Captain Davis inquires.

"No, heavens no. I simply want to have a drink with you both, as real men do. Please, pour yourselves a drink, and take a seat," Mayor Reinhart details.

Captain Davis and Detective Dewalt pour small drinks.

"Gentleman, we must clear the air," Mayor Reinhart says.

Everyone is seated comfortably. Captain Davis and Detective Dewalt are quietly concerned. However, they remain cautiously optimistic.

"This shouldn't come as a surprise. A recent audit of our departments shows we have to seriously begin making cuts across the board," Mayor Reinhart explains.

"When Progressive Task Force 12-Z was created by the former Mayor Riley, longevity was a focal point."

"I understand, sir," Captain Davis replies.

"Progressive Task Force 12-Z earned my respect. All of you had a hand in saving my life. I am forever indebted to all of you brave souls."

"No need to thank us, Mayor Reinhart. We were only doing our jobs," Detective Dewalt chimes in.

"Your job is to make it home safely every night, Detective Dewalt."

"Yes, sir. I understand."

"That goes for you as well, Captain Davis."

"You have my word, Mayor Reinhart."

"My office is the official oversight committee of Progressive Task Force 12-Z. This isn't a tree house operation anymore," Mayor Reinhart elaborates.

Captain Davis and Detective Dewalt sit up in their seats. Finishing both beverages while they sweat in place.

"Money for expanding your unit, and your facility are in the works," Mayor Reinhart says.

Detective Dewalt falls back in his chair. Captain Davis's eyes open wide. Both men stand up immediately thanking the mayor. Almost knocking him over the table from how they approach hugging him.

"Happy to help, gentleman. I am glad you are enthused. I knew this was the right decision."

Detective Dewalt pours up another round of drinks.

"There is one major caveat to all of my bold plans."

"Anything, sir. We are ready, and committed," Captain Davis reassures.

"You must buckle down and exterminate an enemy of the people. Time to pull the plug on, Jake Frunk's game show," Mayor Reinhart commands.

"We won't rest until we do," Detective Dewalt reaffirms.

"Make Jake Frunk's downfall front page news. Finish your investigation within this week," Mayor Reinhart demands.

"You certainly made the right choice, Mayor Reinhart. We will prove ourselves worthy," Captain Davis replies.

"Our futures indefinitely depend on it," Mayor Reinhart confers.

Relishing over the winning news together. A fresh horizon is visible for Captain Davis, and Detective Dewalt. Progressive Task Force 12-Z will be permanent if clues turn up, and the pact doesn't burn up.

"We cannot have this operation going haywire, or we will reap incapacitating repercussions," Mayor Reinhart discerns.

"We will let you know when our investigation is finalized," Captain Davis confirms.

Katrina bursts into the room, holding up an abnormally long sheet of paper. "About your proclamation, Mayor Reinhart ..."

"Oh, yes. My proclamation about tiny homes!"

Detective Dewalt, and Captain Davis see themselves out of Mayor Reinhart's office. Bidding a due to Katrina on the way out. Awaiting on the other side are two law enforcement agents. Each of them flashes their badge. Freezing Captain Davis, and Detective Dewalt in their tracks.

"Captain Davis, and Detective Dewalt, I presume."

"What is happening here?" Captain Davis probes.

"I am Agent Robinson. This is my partner Agent Gonzales from Internal Affairs. We need you gentleman to answer a few questions for us."

Jake Frunk rides along through Chicago. Relaxing, far back in his limousine. Troy's flight is on schedule. The S.S. Marinara presses onward. Activity stretches across every sidewalk. Each business district offers the best from various cultures. Captain Davis, and Detective Dewalt have cause for concern. Time is only a friend when time is working for you.

Autumn leaves glide across the white limousine. Jake Frunk arrives at Mindy's residence. Approaching the gate, Jake Frunk rolls down his window, "Here to see Mindy!"

A security guard is operating the gate from a small booth. Sticking his head out of the window, examining the vehicle.

"Mindy is expecting you," he replies.

The gate opens wide. The operator shuts the window. Jake Frunk rolls up his window as he enters Mindy's premises. Chewing on a biscuit, and then a few crackers with cheese.

Owana is swinging with all of his might, but Detective Reisen is rolling with the punches. Each blast from Owana grazes the shoulders or arms. The crowd is riled up, cheering on the bout. Bonnie is shielding her eyes while attempting to coach her lover in a hail of faith. There is a momentary lapse in judgment when … a body hits the canvas.

Detective Reisen's final combination drops Owana flat on his face. Captain Lockney dives in, and waves off the fight. Owana starts rising but falls back down. Pinchard, throws in the towel, accepting defeat.

A mixture of surrealism, and disbelief keeps the crowd on their feet. Some people tear their betting slips up. A couple storms out furious with the whole scene. A man runs off crying. Complete, and utter chaos is in the driver's seat.

Detective Reisen pauses celebrating until Owana is conscious.

"You have bested me," Owana admits.

"Thank you for giving me the honor of sharing the ring with you, Owana," Detective Reisen replies.

Captain Lockney raises Detective Reisen's hand, "Your winner!" he declares.

The ring is rushed by the crowd. Gobs of people congratulating Detective Reisen, and Owana. Lifting them both in the air. The venue is surpassing maximum capacity as the ruckus crowd hoists both men up high. A true display of emotion, and gratitude for a wonderful show. The cruise line staff works on separating attendees. The crowd shoves back and will not budge. Detective Reisen, and Owana are being paraded through the establishment by a wild bunch.

"Where are we headed?" Detective Reisen inquires.

Owana points ahead at the Tiki Bar. An overbearing crowd places each gentleman on stools. Staff members rush to fill drinks. Two large bubbling beverages are presented.

Owana raises his glass, "Better to drink than to sink."

Detective Reisen raises his glass, and the crowd toasts together.

Bonnie squeezes Detective Reisen and kisses his cheeks a few times. He turns around kissing her lips. Owana notices the display of affection, and smiles. Owana pats Detective Reisen on the back.

"Good show, good friend."

Passengers are gravitating toward the music coming from wide stereo speakers around the Tiki Bar. Serendipity sweeps over the room. A hypnotic sentiment in the air influences smooth dancing. Minds are relaxing and ignoring melodramatic theatrics.

Chapter Eleven: Inside Job

Jake Frunk is escorted into Mindy's lounge. Eric Greitens is seated there. A coffee table is in between them.

"Thanks for joining me, Jake," Mindy says.

Taking a big sip of her coffee.

Jake Frunk's heart beats fast. He overcomes pure shock from seeing Eric Greitens present.

Jake Frunk forces himself to speak, "What are you doing here, Greitens?"

"She ..."

"Don't fret, Jake. I put a retainer out for Eric Greitens. He's the best defense attorney in the City of Chicago," Mindy interrupts.

Eric Greitens glances over at Mindy, and back at Jake Frunk. Anxiously sipping his coffee. Jake Frunk's face hasn't changed.

"She's telling the truth, Jake. We have good news we want to share with you," Greitens contends.

"Please, have a seat, Jake. Pewtrinski is my butler. Please, gather Mr. Frunk some of our delightful coffee."

Pewtrinski motions toward the kitchen.

"No! I don't want any coffee. Let's talk about why I'm here," Jake Frunk barks.

"Have it your way. The hit is off. The cop you want dead poses no threat to your campaign, or us," Mindy explains.

"What kind of operation are you running, Mindy?"

"Jake don't let your emotions get the best of you," Greitens says, calmly, wanting to soothe the situation.

"Looks as if greed got the best of you two. Give me my money back, and don't worry about the hit. You don't have the gull anyhow," Jake Frunk stammers.

"The money is mine. You owe me for the last project of yours that soured downtown. Cost me a fortune in lot rent, and fees," Mindy retorts.

"You selfish slob! This is blackmail!" Jake Frunk rages.

"This makes us even!" Mindy shouts.

"This is for your betterment, Jake!" Greitens snarls.

Two of Mindy's guards rush into the room. Jake Funk stands up and kicks the chair over toward them. Whipping out his pistol and spinning around. Waiting for anyone to test him. Mindy and Eric Greitens rise to their feet. Their hands held high. Pewtrinski takes off running, and hurts his knee.

"Wait! Everything is fine! Please, leave the room, security!" Mindy hollers.

Jake Frunk has a pistol pointed toward both security guards.

"Jake, please, this is a misunderstanding," Greitens pleads.

Jake Frunk holds the gun on the two men. Looking over at Mindy, and Eric Greitens. Glaring at the two security officers, "You heard her, take your leave gentleman."

The two security officers look toward Mindy. One of them speaks up, "Are you sure?"

"Yes, Martel. You, and Damian are excused. Please, return to your posts," Mindy orders.

Martel and Damian have one last look at Jake Frunk before exiting. Jake Frunk lowers his weapon.

"You made a smart decision, Jake. Pass me your gun, and sit down," Greitens coaxes.

"Shut your flap trap, Greitens!" Jake Frunk shouts.

Jake Frunk shoves Eric Greitens to the ground. Pausing, before doing anything drastic. Mindy is flabbergasted as her mouth opens wide in disarray.

"I have a race to win for mayor of this forgotten city!" Jake Frunk waves his pistol around. "You two must decide where you will stand when I do win. Figure out what you truly stand to lose," Jake Frunk finishes.

"We need your word; you won't do anything to jeopardize that policeman's life. It will come back to haunt us," Greitens explains.

"The hit is off, and so is our partnership. Find yourself a new stooge," Jake Frunk replies.

Jake Frunk tucks his firearm away as he walks out of the room. Entering his vehicle and pulling away. A shadow of someone watches carefully in their vehicle from a distance. Downtown, the situation is shaking out strangely for Captain Davis, and Detective Dewalt.

"We overheard, you both are overstepping your bounds," Agent Robinson proposes.

"What are you two after?" Captain Davis asks.

"They must want a raise bad, Captain," Dewalt says.

"Enough of the small talk!" Agent Gonzales shouts.

Agents Gonzales, and Robinson sniff the air.

"You two smell as if you were at the bar!" Agent Gonzales shouts.

"Both of you drunks will tell us what we want to know. What ghost operation do you have going on at this very minute?" Agent Robinson probes.

"Do you believe it is funny to booze up on the job, Captain?" Agent Gonzales inquires.

"Is this a game to you? If you believe this is all a game, I will show you a game!" Agent Robinson howls.

Nearly jumping across the table when Agent Gonzales holds him back. Detective Dewalt jumps out of his chair, nearly swinging at Agent Gonzales. Captain Davis prevents him from doing so.

"You two are going to get my lawyer and cut the act," Captain Davis demands.

"What's wrong, Captain? Are you too good to speak with us?" Agent Robinson asks.

"I am smarter than both of you, bozos. Take your circus to the phone and bring my lawyer in here immediately."

"You appear extremely guilty if you don't answer our questions," Agent Gonzales mocks.

"We will tell you the truth," Detective Dewalt suggests.

"That is much better," Agent Robinson says.

"Confessing to us is good for your career. I applaud your decision to do what's right," Agent Gonzales says.

"The truth is you both are a couple of idiots."

Mayor Reinhart and City Prosecutor Scotch burst into the interrogation room. Right before the situation turns violent.

Both agents scoot back and rise.

"Who do you think you are?" Agent Robinson inquires.

"I'm, Mayor Reinhart. This is City Prosecutor Scotch. Your boss is waiting outside. If you want to keep your job, exit immediately. Your rouse is up."

Agent Robinson stares blindly ahead. Agent Gonzales tugs him by the arm. Both agents scamper out of the room.

"Funny seeing you here," Captain Davis jokes.

Captain Davis and Mayor Reinhart embrace in a hug. Detective Dewalt steps over exchanging pleasantries with City Prosecutor Scotch, and Mayor Reinhart.

"How did you know we were down here?" Captain Davis inquires.

"You owe Katrina for this one," Mayor Reinhart replies.

Detective Dewalt nudges Captain Davis in the arm.

"Since we're all here. Let's enjoy dinner on me. What do you all say?" Mayor Reinhart inquires.

"Count me in," Captain Davis replies.

"I'm always ready for a bite to eat," Scotch states.

"I know a sweet spot. If it's alright with you, Mayor Reinhart?" Detective Dewalt probes.

"Fine with me. Lead the way!"

As the four men depart, echoes from Agents Gonzales, and Robinson being chewed out by their superior ring aloud.

Chapter Twelve:
Ambitions Attract

After the party winds down, Celina is dancing with Owana. Detective Reisen, and Bonnie are doing the waltz.

From behind the bar, Jasper announces, "Last call!"

"What do you say, dearest, shall we venture towards our love nest?" Detective Reisen inquires.

He pecks Bonnie on the lips. Bonnie leans in and kisses Detective Reisen vigorously.

"Look at you two love birds," Celina jokes.

Bonnie blushes, and Detective Reisen smiles. Pulling her in and holding her close.

"Meet me tomorrow at The Fellow Flamingo, and we will catch up. I want all of the details from tonight."

Celina and Bonnie share a long hug.

"I will see you tomorrow," Bonnie agrees.

Celina dances over toward Owana. He is grateful she returned. Detective Reisen, and Bonnie rendezvous at their respective sleeping quarters. Romance turns into relaxation, after hours on end. Time is eviscerated, and constraints are repelled. A night both wanted but couldn't deny needing. Leaving doubt inevitability speechless with vividness filling in hearts of bleakness.

"If this was our forever home, I wouldn't complain," Bonnie says.

Laying across Detective Reisen's chest. Waves from outside can be heard by the loving duo. Soothing the couple as they drift asleep.

Morning comes in the form of lightning, and thunder cracking near their eyes. High winds pressed against the cruise ship. The S.S. Marinara's hardware is being put to the test. Cool air grazes an antique clock on the wall.

"Never too early for breakfast," Detective Reisen says.

Rolling out of bed, and up to his feet.

"What do you say I clean myself up, and we go find grub?"

"Let's clean ourselves up," Bonnie whispers.

She smothers Detective Reisen as they fall backwards. A red heart-shaped bed with angel white sheets breaks their fall.

Troy has landed in Mexico. He spots the green vehicle that Jake Frunk swore would be available. In a few steps, Troy is inside. He fires up the engine. A sound as if the car had seen better days barrels out. Fishing the map out of the glove compartment. After playing the waiting game, Troy enters the long game. Troy cruises toward the marked coordinators before his vehicle bottoms out.

Back in the windy city polls in the race for Mayor of Chicago are tightening. Not close enough to satisfy, Jake Frunk. He loses patience with each passing minute. Pressure on his future business dealings after falling out with, Mindy continues fueling a boiling scorn within him. A downtown last-minute rally provides Jake Frunk a platform to mount an offensive.

"This tool for the machine is not working," Jake begins. He stands before a crowd of hundreds of frustrated citizens. "We need a leader, who is a visionary. A humanitarian, that is ready to beat back ideas from the status quo. The days of economic mutiny are kaput. Chicago will be open for business the moment, I take over!"

A surprisingly large number of people in attendance cheer on, Jake Frunk.

"Current, Mayor Reinhart was put in place by the powers of greed, and misfortune. A special election amid a tragedy. A sham to railroad former, Mayor Riley. She was proven innocent and is owed an apology.

One she is still waiting on. In closing, my final thoughts are final questions. Who is truly the victim here? Is it, Mayor Riley? Is it, Mayor Reinhart? Or is it, you all before me, the residents of Chicago?"

Off in the distance, Captain Davis, and Detective Dewalt examine the scene.

"I don't believe anybody would indulge this conman," Detective Dewalt growls.

"Will see how they act when the dirt flies out on him," Captain Davis states.

A welcoming face steps out from the shadows, "What is our next move?" Suclese inquires.

"Never rush into what will rush after you," Captain Davis relays.

Suclese appears puzzled, "What do you mean?"

"We follow, Jake Frunk," Captain Davis unveils.

Detective Reisen, and Bonnie are almost done with their morning rituals. A storm is adding flair to this loving pair. Chugging along as blue tides rise against the cruise line's sides. In a pursuit for passion fruit, Detective Reisen, and Bonnie are ready to squeeze the juice. An angry storm that won't twist an ample appetite, hungry for more.

Bonnie is in her pink robe while laying out clothes.

"I'm glad you said something about breakfast. I am starving."

She kisses Detective Reisen, before stopping him short of fully dressing.

"I grow hungrier by the minute. That reminds me, I should give, Ray Bongolo a call. Will see if he's ready for our arrival," Detective Reisen details.

Dialing Ray's number, but no dial tone is picked up.

"The signal on the phone is pretty shoddy. I will alert the folks at the front desk."

Detective Reisen refocuses on fixing his public appearance. Grooming himself with a blue comb. He applies moisturizer on his neck and face.

"I will go with you."

Bonnie brushes her hair with a mirror in her line of sight. Sorting through mismatched clothes, but undecided on what to wear.

"Do you believe pink, or blue suits me better?"

"Both colors compliment you well. Whatever you wear, I will be more than satisfied with."

"Let me see ... blue will do!" Bonnie shouts.

Detective Reisen puts flawless finishing touches on his look. Walking towards Bonnie and embracing her. Taking part in an unforgettable moment.

"Have you decided where you want to eat?" Bonnie asks.

"Breakfast is free if we eat in the lobby. If you rather have something different, I am ready to oblige."

"If you are asking, do I want to spend money? Expect my answer to be yes," Bonnie jokes.

They laugh while rocking side to side.

"What did I get myself into?" Detective Reisen asks.

"The time of your life."

Holding hands once they exit their quarters. A few paces and a stretcher become visible. The medical staff is wheeling someone out of their room. As they move closer, Bonnie recognizes a face.

"Dear, Lord. Is that ... Hubert!"

Chapter Thirteen:
Misunderstood

A storm at sea is a sight unseen for a villain blinded by greed. Troy rolls into a small village near the port where he will depart from. Out front is a guard shack with a gate surrounding an entire compound. Troy approaches feeling leery but unfazed.

Troy rolls down his window, "Jake Frunk sent me."

The guard has dark shades on and is in tiger-striped camouflage. A rifle is draped around his neck hanging down to his chest. He nods his head, and points ahead to the compound. He signals to keep driving afterward. Troy nods his head in agreement. Pulling forward, Troy follows bright markings on the ground which guide his way. Entering below the docks behind the compound.

Troy enters the speedboat. Everything is prepared for a voyage. Weapons, coordinates, and a proper tracking system are in place. When Troy arrives at his destination, he may enact a distress beacon. Distracting the Coast Guard, by luring them to his location. From that point, the speedboat will be towed back to shore. If everything goes according to plan, Troy will board the S.S. Marinara before the cruise's final leg of the trip.

"Any sign of him?" Captain Davis asks, over the radio.

"No sign. Lost him for now," Detective Dewalt responds.

"Circle and try a different street. He's up to something," Captain Davis demands.

"Yes, sir. Circling now," Detective Dewalt says.

Suclese is in the passenger seat monitoring traffic. Detective Dewalt scours alleyways, and side streets for any sign of Jake Frunk.

"I am extremely glad you could meet with me, Golden One," Jake Frunk admonishes.

"Not a problem, Jake. You haven't caused me any trouble."

The Golden One eats his steak dinner slowly. Enjoying each bite atop the rooftop of his home.

"Your businesses haven't helped our family much, but that can be solved in a city this big."

"I am glad you see things that way, Golden One."

Golden One chomps down on another few bites of steak. Jake Frunk has barely touched his food.

"Mindy says, you lost your cool the other day. She's my daughter, and I know she can be a pain. However, she's a grown woman, and next in line to secede me. Your best interest is to never let this happen again."

"Certainly, sir. Golden One, sir. I lost my cool. I am not that type of person."

"I know you aren't, Jake. I wouldn't have invested as much in you as I have if I believed you would be a nuisance."

"Thank you. The real reason—"

"The real reason you are here is because you're in a bind. You need money, and your campaign is bogging down," Golden One interjects.

"That's all true, but ... I have a plan."

"The problem is your plans are what carried you into this mess. A man isn't judged by what he has, but instead, by what he doesn't have," Golden One explains.

He finishes devouring a juicy tender steak until only bones are left.

"I don't have any more money for you, Jake. You owe me for the dinner as well. This whole Mayor of Chicago business is way above your comprehension skill level."

Jake flips the table over knocking the Golden One down. Golden One pulls out his gun, but Jake Frunk boots it away. They wrestle over the weapon. Kicking, clawing, and biting for dear life. After rolling too far over, Golden One falls from the rooftop. Jake Frunk is barely hanging on to the ledge before pulling himself up to safety.

Golden One's body lays waste below. Indented into a car's hood. On the same street, Detectives Dewalt, and Suclese begin driving down.

"Captain Davis, you must have a look at this," Detective Dewalt radios over.

"I cannot help, but believe someone attempted to kill poor, Hubert," Bonnie worries.

"Maybe, food poisoning. I'm sorry either way. What would someone gain from Hubert's death?" Celina probes.

"That is what I don't comprehend," Bonnie relinquishes.

"What did the doctor say in the medical bay?"

"Hubert will live and make a full recovery. However, he must be on bed rest for a few days," Bonnie relays.

"I am sorry, sweetie. The only thing I recall, was his mean fiancée tossing a drink in his face," Celina states.

"Such a shame. Hubert is a true gentleman. Hubert mentioned that his fiancée didn't return to their room until after late last night. Long after dinner was finished."

"Takes her out of the picture," Celina begrudges.

"For the time being," Bonnie retorts.

"Do you believe shopping would free our minds?"

"Sure. When doesn't shopping help?" Bonnie inquires.

"I will close up the bookstore and meet you out front."

After visiting a few stores, Celina spots something from the corner of her eyes. Her orange and white striped cat named Crush is on the loose. and running wild. With only a few bags in their possession, both women race after Crush.

Captain Lockney bumps into Detective Reisen near the bathroom, "I've been meaning to tell you something."

"What's wrong?" Detective Reisen inquires.

"A man was found dead near the casino last night. We haven't found any leads."

"Have any witnesses spoken out?" Detective Reisen asks.

"None came forward," Captain Lockney replies.

"Do you believe his death was an accident?"

"Do you believe lighting can strike the same place twice?" Captain Lockney probes.

"You make a valid point. I will keep my eyes peeled," Detective Reisen states.

Detective Reisen walks into a lounge where free breakfast is wrapping up. While snagging a bite to eat, Detective Reisen notices a woman acting suspiciously. Peering around frantically through her glasses. Giving off the impression she is hiding something, or fearful of someone. Brushing it off, and continuing eating. Detective Reisen makes a mental tab of which direction she is heading. Including, what she is wearing.

When Detective Reisen peers the opposite way, Bonnie, and Celina are running. Drawing his attention away he quickly stands up. He sees the orange, and white striped cat being chased. In a matter of seconds, Detective Reisen joins in the race.

Captain Davis arrives at the crime scene. Detectives Dewalt, and Suclese have yellow tape outlined around the area. Onlookers from the neighborhood line the streets.

"Not a good scene," Suclese utters.

"May take a few days before we know what building he fell off of, but we will find out," Detective Dewalt states.

"No coincidence detected," Suclese presumes.

"Not even the slightest bit," Captain Davis attributes.

Jake Frunk continues his warpath after escaping the clutches of Progressive Task Force 12-Z. He stalks Mindy's residence until a vehicle exits. After turning a corner Jake Frunk rams his car into Mindy's limousine. Jake Frunk opens the driver-side door Pewtrinski, is driving. Jake Frunk, shoots Pewtrinski, point blank.

Pressing the unlock button for every door before Jake Frunk swings around to the back. Opening a random door and attempting to execute Mindy. However, she has vanished. Jake Frunk is shocked and looks around for her.

Another vehicle shoots off down the road. Flames fire out of all cylinders. Jake Frunk is firing shots at the back of the vehicle. Returning to his car and driving off as if nothing happened.

Chapter Fourteen: A Cat And A Cure

"There you are poor, kitty!" Celina unloads. Grasping Crush, the cat, in her hands. "Thank you so much, you both. Without your help, I may never have been able to keep Crush from being hurt."

"Glad we could assist," Detective Reisen says. "Don't let me hold you both up. Enjoy shopping without me for a while."

Detective Reisen kisses Bonnie with extra sugar before walking away.

"He is truly, a good man," Celina praises.

"Glad we both agree," Bonnie replies.

Detective Reisen steps outside for a taste of fresh air. A man in a silver-tone suit is holding a book and looking over the edge. Detective Reisen grabs a refreshment and stands next to a glowing gentleman.

"Ocean waters are calm after a storm. Once, a storm has been gone long enough, the waves return to their old habits."

"Extremely prophetic, old timer," Detective Reisen says.

"Please, forgive me. As you can see, years have aged better than my manners."

"What are you going on about?"

"My name is, Mr. Platinum."

"Glad we became acquainted. Call me, Detective Reisen."

Both men shake hands. Detective Reisen smells booze all over Mr. Platinum.

"A detective, you say. What city do you serve?"

"The great City of Chicago," Detective Reisen replies.

"Nearly have to be a criminal to arrest anyone there."

"You are quite funny, Mr. Platinum. What line of work are you in?" Detective Reisen inquires.

"Line of work. My dearest, son, I am in the cruise line business."

"Oh, that must be a treat."

"The real treat is owning a ship of your own."

"There is a dream, I will propose a toast to."

"Not a dream, son. The S.S. Marinara is mine."

Detective Reisen spits out his drink over the ledge.

"Do you own this cruise ship?"

"Aye, now, you have matured in front of my very eyes."

"That is impressive, by any stretch of the imagination."

"Time wouldn't cease, so opportunity I seized. For me to stretch across the seven seas," Mr. Platinum says.

"You are a quality storyteller as well."

"Remember, you don't need a royal flush to win. You need a greater bluff," Mr. Platinum suggests.

"Makes perfect sense."

"We are living in an age of noise. Your purpose is today!"

"I will take your food for thought into consideration. Thank you, for your words of wisdom," Reisen commends.

"See you around, sometime. I have a brother in Chicago."

Mr. Platinum makes his exit. A plaque with a poem droop on the wall before the door leads back inside. The Poem of Hearts reads, 'Where many hearts are called away, a bigger heart is called upon. Will the storm overtake us? If we last, will cuts on our hearts enrage us? If our faith is kept, will the gust shake us?'

Detective Reisen studies the Poem of Hearts a few times, before heading back inside. Captain Lockney is fast approaching him.

"Good to see you, Detective Reisen. Unfortunately, I come bearing another round of bad news."

"What's wrong, Captain Lockney?"

"The brown-haired man you were wrestling with in the lobby, has succumbed to his injuries."

"Sorry to hear. Where do we go from here?"

"I am in your corner, detective. He was out of line. For now, enjoy your cruise aboard the S.S. Marinara."

"Are you certain?" Detective Reisen inquires.

"I have full confidence in my decision-making, detective. You made the right decision, but please, respect mine. By the look of things, he was suffocated to death anyhow."

Captain Lockney places his hand on Detective Reisen's shoulder. They exchange a look in perpetuity before Captain Lockney disappears.

Detective Reisen glances over at the Poem of Hearts one last time. Progressing further down the hall. He spots the woman who was acting strange from earlier near the lounge. The S.S. Mariniara begins porting, before the final stretch of the cruise. Where the cruise ship will turn around and begin heading back to the City of Tampa Bay.

Troy begins ascending onboard.

After a few steps, "Stop right where you are at!"

Two security guards are rushing toward, Troy. The first security guard attempts tackling, him. Troy knocks him unconscious, with an elbow to the back of his head. Another security guard is using mace on Troy, but he punches the spray out of his clutches. Shoving the security guard into the edge of the ship, where Troy flips him into the water below.

"Swim back, so I can beat you again," Troy mocks.

"Hey, punk! You messed up big time!" Owana shouts.

Troy stops in his tracks, and turns around, "Nobody is going to apologize. Keep stepping before you get hurt."

"You don't appear strong enough to hurt me. Take your leave, before you don't have a choice," Owana replies.

"Looks, as if you were already whooped. I will whoop you a second time," Troy declares.

Troy rushes forward and squares up with Owana.

Detective Reisen notices a set of televisions in the long, beige-colored hall. A bright red banner says breaking news on one of the television screens. Peering closer at a street in Chicago. A woman named, Mindy, and her chauffeur named Pewtrinski were attacked by a gunman. Pewtrinski is in critical condition, but Mindy was able to fend off the attacker, before escaping death. Detective Reisen scratches his chin and continues on his path.

Chicago is calm at the present moment. Jake Frunk is on the move, and some would say the run. Progressive Task Force 12-Z is hungry for expansion. Each officer is ready to pay their dues. At a shared headquarters inside the precinct, they work tirelessly on a ploy to gain a step on, Jake Frunk.

Captain Davis sits behind an enormous mahogany wooden desk, "He's going to strike again soon."

"How fast, and where?" Detective Dewalt inquires.

Suclese walks over and flips on the evening news. The broadcast announces, that Chicago is under a dark cloud today. Not long after an attempted double homicide, another man fell from a rooftop. A news ticker running below reads Progressive Task Force 12-Z is hot on the case.

"Wonderful work, Suclese," Captain Davis obliges.

Bonnie and Celina are finishing their final tour of the cruise ship.

"Are you going to spill the beans about last night?"

"Ha! You beat me to asking first. A woman never kisses, and tells," Bonnie replies.

"Don't tell me, you are too good for me already."

"I won't," Bonnie jokes.

"Funny, but you write about serious topics."

"I write what's in my heart. Let's grab something to eat at this place up ahead. I will fill you in on every detail."

"That is what I need to hear!" Celina hollers.

"I need to hear, what you were doing last night as well. This isn't a one-way street," Bonnie contends.

Bonnie and Celina laugh while capitulating pillow talk, over a late lunch. Outside of gossip, more than a food fight is brewing. Both brutes are tied up on their feet. Owana slips in a few uppercuts, and a jab before they briefly separate.

Security runs past where Detective Reisen is located. He follows close behind. Troy nearly trips Owana, but falls face-first when Owana shifts his body weight. Giving himself a clear advantage. Troy wraps his arms around Owana's waist and drives him backward against the edge.

Security is closing in. Detective Reisen passes them up on the way to stop the fight. Owana peers at everyone and pulls Troy over the side with him. Detective Reisen extends his arms out to catch him. Chief of Security, Roberto, radios in for a rescue team to begin descending. Time will run short on finding the men who went overboard. Security works all night to no end. Roberto and another man have to hold Detective Reisen back from diving in after Owana.

Bonnie and Celina watch carefully as Hubert's fiancée walks past them. She is high stepping toward the medical bay. Hubert is fast asleep, as she reaches his bed. She drops a few splashes of something into Hubert's drink. Before she can put it away, Celina enters with her phone camera out filming the entire scene. "Stop what you're doing!" she shouts.

"This is his medicine!"

She tries running away, but Bonnie tackles her down to the floor. "Citizen's arrest!" Bonnie shouts.

Detective Reisen and a few securities guards rush in.

"What's happening here, ladies?" Detective Reisen asks.

"She tried poising that poor man. I have it all on video."

"I swear I wasn't doing anything wrong!"

"Beatrice, how could you?" Hubert whines.

"You will need to come with me," Roberto states.

Bonnie, and Celina hand Beatrice over to security.

"My name is Roberto, Chief of Security."

"I know who you are, Roberto. I work here as well," Celina states.

"Oh! Dang! You're right. I need to obtain all the evidence from you, please. If you ladies will accompany me to sign a witness statement, I would be much obliged."

"Lead the way, Roberto!" Celina hollers.

"Great work you two!" Detective Reisen shouts.

Detective Reisen kisses, Bonnie while squeezing her.

"You arere holding me as if something is wrong."

"Something is wrong, dearest. Owana has fallen off."

"Do you mean, he fell off of the cruise?" Bonnie probes.

"Yes, love. Security is searching for him now. The Coast Guard will take responsibility after too long."

"I am sorry, dear," Bonnie says.

"Sorry to interrupt," Hubert begins. Drying his eyes with a handkerchief. "You mean, that fella you boxed earlier, fell off of the S.S. Marinara?"

"Yes, Hubert. Owana was attacked by another man. Unfortunately, both of them plunged below," Reisen states.

"Sorry, for your loss. Sad to say, this makes me feel better about my present condition," Hubert relays. Scooping up his beverage, trying not to let tears slip in his drink.

"Stop! Don't drink that! It's poison!" Bonnie shouts.

Hours pass by, and neither Troy nor Owana have turned up. The crew member who went overboard appears to have suffered a similar fate. The S.S. Marinara pulls anchor and continues. One last stop until Detective Reisen and Bonnie Butterfield step off.

Chapter Fifteen: Switch Up Luck

Bonnie, and Detective Reisen return to their room. She senses he is not himself.

"Here! Take this!"

Bonnie passes a coffee with a shot of liquor in it, "You are stressed this will help."

She rubs his shoulders as he takes a sip.

"How does this happen?" Detective Reisen inquires.

"Because we can't fix everything all of the time."

She kisses Detective Reisen along his neck. Embracing, and easing his strain.

"You were strong in the ring," Bonnie suggests.

"Strong ... more dumb than strong to take on a big ogre that size."

"You won in front of all those people who bet against you. Have more pride in your accomplishment."

"Some of those folks who wagered on me made off with more than my yearly salary," Detective Reisen counters.

"None of them earned a free cruise," Bonnie contends.

She kisses Detective Reisen on his chest up to his neck. He smiles while kissing Bonnie for a few moments longer.

"You may be right. However, nobody wins when two people fight," Detective Reisen states.

"I believe someone always wins in a fight!"

Bonnie kisses Detective Reisen excitedly as minutes turn into hours. Bonnie's hand runs along his jawline. They feel love, and a powerful connection between them.

"Hard to be motivated when a man you fought fairly, ends up walking the plank," Detective Reisen confesses.

"You both made the same agreement. Owana would want you to be happy. Celina will be devastated, but we don't have to be at this moment."

Bonnie gives Detective Reisen a look of encouragement. He pulls her close as passion ensues, and the lights shut off. Mornings can be heavy, but a person who avoids them will be left in the dark. Knocking on the door wakes the couple up. Detective Reisen makes it to the door and sees Hubert standing there.

"Hello, Hubert. Is everything alright?"

"Not exactly. If you don't mind, would you come with me?" Hubert inquires.

"Certainly. Spare me a moment to throw something appropriate on."

"Hello, Hubert!" Bonnie shouts.

Hubert waves before Detective Reisen shuts the door to address his wardrobe. Trouble around the corner is constantly waiting for you in a big city. Jake Frunk is on the minds of many, but in the hearts of plenty who wish him dead.

"He murdered my father, and nearly took my life. Pewtrinski, may end up a vegetable because of that animal. Bring me, Jake Frunk's head on a golden platter!" Mindy screams.

Mindy stands before her collective of minions. Including, Eric Greitens.

"Wait a minute. Please," Greitens pleads.

Everyone turns their attention to him.

"How are you sure, Jake Frunk killed your father, then attacked you, and Pewtrinski?"

Mindy steps down from the counter and comes face to face with Eric Greitens. Slapping him in the face, and kicking him in the gut, "Never speak unless spoken to, slug!"

Mindy grabs Eric Greitens by his jacket and pulls him close, "I saw Jake Frunk out for blood with my own eyes. Then my life flashed before mine. You will watch him die in front of yours!"

"Do you need me to tag along?" Bonnie asks.

"No, baby. This is a man-to-man thing," Reisen replies.

He kisses Bonnie goodbye for the time being.

"I promise not to keep him long," Hubert jokes.

"Don't worry about it," Bonnie says.

Detective Reisen, and Hubert, walk a great distance before anybody speaks.

"Where are you taking me, Hubert?"

"Not much further," Hubert replies.

Arriving at what appears to be a brig of some sort.

"We're here," Hubert states.

"Where exactly are we?"

"Where they are holding my fiancée, Beatrice."

"Oh, I see. What is your angle, Hubert?"

"Man-to-man, I am not certain if I should press charges. What should I do, Detective Reisen?"

"If it were me deciding, Hubert, I wouldn't want anybody poisoning me."

"Maybe, she was nervous."

"Nervous ... nervous about what?"

"Maybe, she didn't believe I would support her after falling ill."

"Hubert, she was the reason you were sick!"

Hubert paces back, and forth. Biting his finger in frustration, "I don't know. I don't believe it."

Detective Reisen throws his arm over Hubert's shoulder. They begin walking, and Reisen begins, "I understand, you don't want to believe she can cause harm, Hubert. Being honest with yourself is the most important thing a man can do."

"I am being honest. Truly with all my heart I am being sincere. I am so confused!"

"What happens when you go to eat, or drink something, but nobody is around to save you? Are you willing to take that risk?"

"I need more time to consider."

"Think long, and hard about it. Hubert, you may not have this opportunity again."

Detective Reisen continues walking away, leaving Hubert standing in his self-pity.

"Wait!" Hubert shouts.

He sprints toward Detective Reisen.

"I know you weren't poisoned that fast, Hubert."

"No. I have been feeling better since we last spoke. Thank you for opening my eyes back there. I was in love, but truly, I wanted to be in love," Hubert reveals.

"Yes, my good friend Hubert. Love is a dangerous game."

"You aren't lying, detective. Should I say, goodbye? I hate to leave on these terms."

"Beatrice said, goodbye. A long time ago, Hubert."

"You are probably right about that as well."

"Allow me to share something with you. This is the last night before we take our leave. If you want, you may join us when we depart. We are staying with a good friend of mine. Plenty of room, and free of distractions. What do you say?"

"What a stupendous idea. If I stay aboard the S.S. Marinara, I will long for Beatrice harder."

"You are healing my friend but healing fast. Are you up for some air hockey?" Detective Reisen inquires.

"Will playing air hockey speed up the healing process?"

"Ha-ha! Until I win," Detective Reisen jokes.

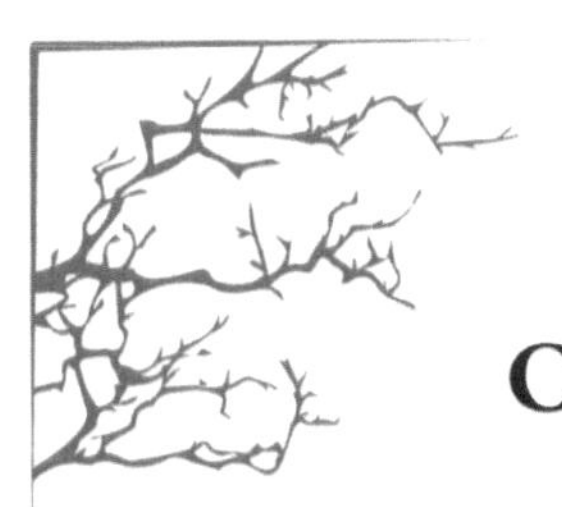

Chapter Sixteen:
Election's Eve

Final polls tighten as do the strings holding up Jake Frunk. Trying not to drink himself into an abyss while plotting his next course of action. Jake Frunk's window of becoming Mayor of Chicago is sliding closed. He is having trouble sitting still let alone clearing his consciousness. Ambitions and desires find themselves on the brink of imploding.

Jake Frunk's mind is overloading. Time is ticking while his life and dreams hang in the balance. Finishing a bottle off while feeling his life may be on the line. With nothing left to lose, but his behind.

Bonnie is on the way to meet Celina. Figuring out how to break the news concerning, Owana's apparent passing. The Fellow Flamingo is open for business as Bonnie enters.

"Hey! Glad you made it!" Celina hollers.

Sweeping around the counter, and hugging Bonnie.

"Good to see you as well. Do you have a minute to talk?"

"Sure, Bonnie. What's wrong?"

"This is regarding, Owana."

"What happened to the big fighting man I was getting my groove on with last night?" Celina asks.

"Sorry, Celina. Owana fell off of the ship."

Celina reaches out and holds Bonnie's arms. They shed tears together before Celina returns to her counter. Celina counts down her cash register drawer. She places the money in her safe.

"How about a drink?"

"I'd appreciate that a lot right now, Bonnie."

Celina cries, and Bonnie rushes over to hug her again.

Captain Davis is in a vehicle down the road from Jake Frunk's property. Detectives Dewalt, and Suclese are in a squad car on an adjacent side street.

"Haven't seen anything yet," Detective Dewalt states.

"We've only been here a few hours. Give it time, something will happen tonight," Captain Davis reassures.

"We will stay focused," Detective Dewalt responds.

"What do you believe will happen?" Suclese inquires.

"Exactly what you are seeing now," Dewalt suggests.

"You may be right, but Captain Davis believes something will undoubtedly happen," Seleucus rebuttals.

"Captain Davis has been watching too much Film Noir. There is no way any goons would attack this goof's home."

"What makes you believe that?" Suclese probes.

"Jake Frunk is running for mayor. Although, he is a criminal, attacking him would be uncharacteristic during an election. May even send him over the edge."

"Where do your beliefs stem from?" Suclese inquires.

"The caliber of a criminal is how fast they retaliate. The faster a criminal retaliates the more likely he or she is sloppy unprofessional."

"An sloppy unprofessional crook! Where do you come up with this stuff?" Suclese probes.

"We will put my theory to the test!"

Captain Davis chuckles.

"How will we accomplish that?" Suclese inquires.

"If these perpetrators show up, we will see if they are savages or sophisticated killers," Detective Dewalt explains.

"Sophisticated, do you mean as in a knife, and a fork?" Captain Davis asks.

"Sophisticated, meaning they cover their tracks well," Detective Dewalt elaborates.

An eerie mist hovers around their vehicles. Cool air mixed with high humidity is causing a spooky ambiance. Fog rolls in from Lake Michigan as red ferns blow in the field they idle by.

"A few cars are pulling into the alleyway," Captain Davis announces.

Detectives Dewalt, and Suclese peer ahead. Counting three cars creeping toward, Jake Frunk's lair.

"Savages!" Detective Dewalt belts out.

"Move in fast and make some noise! Backup is on the way," Captain Davis relays.

Detective Dewalt parks the car in a position blocking an exit. Captain Davis blocks the other end. The perpetrators have the barrels of their guns aiming through the fence's gaps. They are moments away from incapacitating Jake Frunk.

"Stop, or we will shoot!" Captain Davis shouts.

Sirens are blaring as weapons are drawn by all parties. Some men start shooting through the fence at Jake Frunk's home. Other men jump back in their vehicles to try and escape.

A vehicle attempts to run over Detectives Dewalt, and Suclese. They fire shots into the vehicle before they can be rundown. A few men fall into the fetal position succumbing to their wounds. A driver is shot by Captain Davis when he opens the door firing back.

The last remaining vehicle attempts to leave but reverses into a brick wall. The airbag goes off, and the driver is smashing it down. Pulling his car around, and narrowly missing Captain Davis. Ramming into a wall again, but this time, the driver stops moving.

"Are you both alright?" Captain Davis asks.

Suclese is shaking, "I am fine, Captain."

"Still in one piece," Detective Dewalt conveys.

Jake Frunk exits his home as he has a great gander around the scene, "Big mess to clean up."

Jake Frunk sips his bottle as he returns inside.

In the bedroom with candles lit, and water streaming into the hot tub. Detective Reisen, and Bonnie Butterfield find their way into a lover's hidden gem. A special retreat which provides ultimate relief. Weather is perking up on their final day aboard the S.S. Marinara.

"Are you fond of anything from our trip?"

"I love that we are sharing this moment," Bonnie replies.

She locks lips and kisses Detective Reisen softly. They slide into the hot tub.

"Wow! Hot! Hot! Hot water!" Detective Reisen shouts.

"Sorry, it's not an ice bath," Bonnie jousts.

"Perfectly, fine. I'm not prepared to do a polar plunge, quite yet."

Bonnie giggles while sliding into the water. She cuddles up with her lover in a corner of the hot tub. Rose petals in the water with a French vanilla scent in the air. Not a care in the world for this loving pair.

Rain smacks off the pavement in Chicago while temperatures are unusually warm. People are casting their final ballots in the city's election for mayor. A four-year term will be awarded to the winner. Many other initiatives and city-wide government positions are up for a vote. Not only is current Mayor Reinhart's political career on the table, but the future of Progressive Task Force 12-Z is as well.

With results piling in at an unprecedented rate, the counting of ballots will take well into the next morning. A winner may not be decided soon, and this could head for a run-off election. Jake Frunk watches from his election headquarters, downtown at the Funky Scooter Palace. His supporters are confident and cheering in full force. Results pit Jake Frunk in the lead while Detective Reisen and Bonnie dig into the main course.

Current Mayor Reinhart watches with Progressive Task Force 12-Z in full attendance—minus Detective Reisen. Air is thinning, and the atmosphere is depreciating. Hope may be all that remains as Jake Frunk starts pulling further away with an early lead.

"Do you believe Jake has a chance to win?" Greitens asks.

"Jake Frunk has zero shot of winning this election," Mindy replies, switching off the television.

"I understand. Mindy, I have been meaning to speak with you about the legal side of business since your father has passed away."

"We will talk about my father's legal matters when I feel the time is right."

"I agree. This is a bad time. However, this is about your legal matters, Mindy."

"What did you say?" Mindy probes.

"Your father signed over his estate to me. My name is on the deed to this property, and all of his properties."

Eric Greitens hands Mindy a golden binder of deeds.

"Here are each of the copies," Greitens states.

Mindy tosses the binder at Eric and begins assaulting him. Punching, and kicking him until he trips over the coffee table. His body hits the ground making a loud thudding sound. All of the commotion alerts more security guards.

"Get out of my house!" Mindy shouts.

Eric Greitens escapes to the kitchen. Mindy raises her small handgun and fires off a few shots. Eric Greitens is taking cover. Both security guards, Damian, and Martel work to stop Mindy from killing Eric Greitens.

Eric rises up to his feet, "No, Mindy. That is where you are wrong," Greitens smirks.

Eric Greitens wipes blood away from his lip, "These security guards are employed by me. Get out of my house!"

Mindy attacks security before they lift her off of the ground. Struggling to drag her away. Mindy kicks, spits, and screams at them. Clawing them while attempting to pry their eyes out each chance she receives.

"I will have my revenge!" Mindy vows.

Chapter Seventeen: NBS

"Wake up! Sugar! Wake up!" Bonnie shouts.

She shakes Detective Reisen out of a deep sleep.

"What's wrong? What's wrong, dear?"

"He won! He did it!"

"Who won? What did they do? What did they win?"

"Reinhart! Mayor Reinhart won!"

Detective Reisen rolls out of bed, "That old dog learned a new trick!"

Kissing Bonnie before prancing around the room. A knock at the door interrupts the celebration. Detective Reisen opens the door quickly. Awaiting is a friendly face.

"Did I pop in at a bad time?" Celina asks.

"No way!" Bonnie shouts.

She runs up and pulls Celina inside to dance with her.

"Whoa! What's the celebration about?" Celina probes.

"Our good friend won his election for mayor, technically reelection," Bonnie elaborates.

"No time for a technical analysis, victory is victory," Detective Reisen states.

"Time to party!" Bonnie shouts.

Detective Reisen turns up the music's volume. Another knock at the door interrupts magnified multiplied merriment. Detective Reisen stares through the peephole confused by the visitor's arrival. Bonnie, and Celina appear highly curious.

"Hey, Hubert. How are you?" Detective Reisen inquires.

Hubert stands in the doorway with two bottles of champagne.

"I feel better. Thank you all. Am I interrupting anything?"

"No. Please, step inside, Hubert" Detective Reisen says.

Hubert sets his bottles of champagne down on a counter.

"Hello, Hubert. Glad to see you. Would you please, turn up the music a little more?" Bonnie asks.

"Happy to see you as well. Certainly, I will raise the volume for you. I don't believe we've been properly introduced," Hubert decrees.

"Hubert, this is Celina," Bonnie introduces.

"Hubert is an avid reader," Celina says.

"Oh! Yes! You're quite right. How embarrassing. I bought a book from your shop a few days ago. Please, forgive me. I am going through a rather difficult time," Hubert unveils.

"Bonnie, and I did witness Mister Boxer over there, take down a monster while accompanying you," Celina details.

"My mind is all out of whack. Please, forgive me. I feel terrible for the poor fella, an unequivocal tragedy."

"You are forgiven, Hubert. How is the book you purchased, The Blue Lizard by Silver Toad?" Celina inquires.

"A monumental read! Thank you for your outstanding service, and recommendation, Celina."

"You're welcome, Hubert. Glad I was a big help. Bonnie, there is something I must mention. I put in for a vacation with my time accumulated. I am taking you up on your offer."

"Wonderful! We truly have a reason to celebrate."

Hubert unwraps a champagne bottle. Detective Reisen finishes laying out glasses filled with ice. Holding up the bottle.

"Do you mind if I do the honors?" Hubert asks.

"Please, be my guest," Detective Reisen replies.

Celina, and Bonnie dance with full glasses in hand. Everyone partakes in drinking refreshments.

"On the morning news, I heard your friend, Luis Reinhart won his election for mayor," Hubert states.

"I am proud of Luis," Detective Reisen responds.

"We're proud of him," Bonnie chimes in.

Detective Reisen puts his arm around Bonnie. Everyone takes in the good nature of the moment. Hubert uncorks another bottle of champagne. Bonnie, and Celina clap their hands, and stomp their feet along to the music. Everyone's cups are replenished.

"Would you care to lead us in a toast, Hubert?" Bonnie inquires.

"On second thought, I would appreciate it if your fiancé' did the honors," Hubert suggests.

"Very well then. Cheers to a vacation, after a vacation," Detective Reisen toasts.

Raising his glass as everyone else does. In the name of a celebration of good times, and great company.

A small house with trees around it lies outside of Chicago's city limits. Sitting across the state line in Indiana. There are no vehicles in the driveway as Jake Frunk pulls up. Exiting his vehicle and walking up to the door. Leaves blow all around as the wind grows stronger on a merciless early afternoon. Bright sunlight gives off exuberant amounts of heat, and humidity is extraordinarily high.

Detective Reisen escorts Bonnie, Celina, and Hubert out of the room. The party stops, and Detective Reisen exchanges pleasantries with Captain Lockney before stepping back on shore. All essentials are packed, and no one is giving them flack.

"They said be out by eleven o'clock, and we beat them by fifteen minutes," Detective Reisen boasts.

Detective Reisen spots Ray Bongolo waiting in his Humvee. Bongolo Enterprise is painted on the side. He waves for the party to head over.

"You brought a few extras," Ray Bongolo observes.

"Tried to call, and let you know. Hope you don't mind," Detective Reisen states.

"Not at all. I will help you fit their luggage inside. We're waiting on one more person," Ray Bongolo states.

"What do you mean one more person? No. Ray, buddy, this is everyone," Detective Reisen reassures.

"Forgot to mention, my fiancée, Beatrice was on the cruise with you. My memory is messing with me nowadays," Ray Bongolo explains.

Detective Reisen's face nearly turns pure white. Celina and Bonnie's eyes are larger than the ocean. Hubert barfs over the railing. Crawling out of Ray Bongolo's Humvee onto his knees. Sobbing his heart, and soul out.

"What happened? Please, someone, tell me what happened to Beatrice?"

Detective Reisen steps forward and looks Ray Bongolo square in his confused gaze.

"Beatrice found herself in a bit of trouble. She was Hubert's fiancée as well."

Ray Bongolo's head points toward the ground, as Detective Reisen comforts him.

"I won't cry, buddy. I don't have any tears left," Ray Bongolo says.

Detective Reisen gives him a strong hug. Bonnie and Celina tend to Hubert's emotional distress.

After everyone's luggage is squared away, and hatchets are buried. They head down a beaten path. Driving across dirt, and sand for a few miles. Traversing toward a massive complex.

The air is easy to breathe. A cool breeze puts everyone at ease. Wind picks up in Chicago as a storm rolls in on the parade. Jake Frunk continues walking toward the door of an isolated homestead in Indiana.

Jake Frunk knocks once, and the door swiftly opens.

"Right on time, Jake. Please, have a seat," Greitens says.

Holding the door open is disgraced former Mayor Riley.

"An honest pleasure seeing you again, Mr. Frunk."

Jake Frunk overcomes rash impulses, and deep sudden impact, "Good to see you both. Sorry, about the other day."

"The past was forged, and all is forgotten," Greitens says.

Jake Frunk nods his head while sitting on a black suede sofa. Former Mayor Riley sits across from Jake Frunk on a brown recliner. Eric Greitens sits parallel to them forming a triangle. A glass table with a wooden base is between them. An envelope displaying Jake Frunk's name sits atop the table.

"How do you feel about running for Mayor once more?" Greitens asks.

"The timing is off for me," Jake Frunk admits.

"You nearly won," Riley coaxes.

"I will pass but thank you both for supporting me."

"Thank you for being honest, Jake. What about you former Mayor Riley?" Greitens probes.

"The mayor position is something I have left in the past. We both know the water is a tad bit tainted for another swim. I appreciate your sentiment, Eric Greitens."

"You took over for a corrupt double-crossing lunatic. I'd say, you did a good job of patching things up before Progressive Task Force 12-Z ran you off," Greitens unleashes.

"No thank you," Riley insists.

"What a shame, you were one of the good ones," Greitens confesses.

"Why don't you consider throwing your hat in the race on the next ballot, Greitens?"

"That's a valid question, Jake. I have been modulating, and we don't need the mayor's office. The Mayor and the City of Chicago will need us sooner than anticipated," Greitens suggests.

Shores taste crystal clear water. Dolphins are jumping, and seagulls soar with eagles. At Ray Bongolo's complex, everyone is utilizing each amenity. Ray Bongolo is on a wave rider, showing off on his many floating ramps. Hubert and Celina egg him on. Hubert tosses a log on the fire, which is roasting the meats. Ray Bongolo's compound emits enough light to stretch for over a mile. Detective Reisen drives a wave rider while Bonnie jet skis off of the back.

Activities wind down as darkness descends over the tranquil view. Detective Reisen, and Bonnie make it ashore. Ray Bongolo is right behind the couple. Everyone gathers near the fire as a small radio plays serene music. Relaxing notes bubbling out of the speakers.

"Other than the chaotic nature of events, how was the cruise experience?" Ray Bongolo asks.

"Unforgettable," Detective Reisen replies.

They both smile and assist in filling drinks. A lot of food is cooking up, and everyone is eating shortly.

"There is one thing I can't put my finger on," Celina says.

"What is that?" Bonnie probes.

"They never announced the killer of that man near the casino," Celina finishes.

"Oh, what a calculated observation. You're right!" Hubert shouts.

"I have a hunch on who murdered him," Detective Reisen whispers.

"Who is your best guess, Detective Reisen?" Ray Bongolo inquires.

"Doesn't matter much, now. He is no longer with us."

"You don't think ...," Bonnie shutters.

"He wouldn't!" Hubert shouts.

Celina drops her plate of food, "That explains a lot."

Thousands of people line the streets. Bands march to the sound of each thumping beat. Mayor Reinhart has defended his honor and is assuming the throne of Chicago. A true friend, Luis Reinhart is. Far from a square, he will soar where others show fear. Mayor Reinhart stands over the microphone in a red suit, black undershirt, with a sky-blue tie.

"Thank you all for showing up. The path to victory wouldn't have been paved without you. To my opponent, and nemesis, Jake Frunk, I wish him all the best. I truly do. The smart deserving individuals of this grand city have spoken! They voted for higher wages, a business-friendly environment, and safer neighborhoods. Don't worry about my story, focus on our story!"

The crowd goes bonkers as Mayor Reinhart remains determined to finish his speech.

"We have become hardened when we need to become humble. For my latest decree, fireworks are legal any time of year on Lake Shore Drive!"

The crowd erupts, chanting, and cheering. Fireworks begin blasting into the sky above. Mayor Reinhart fist bumps the air. Overtaken by emotion and encapsulated with divine devotion. Mayor Reinhart's firework pedigree is poised to generate income. A slice of liberty out of an age of gloom.

Chapter Eighteen:
Perpetual Motions

Flying out of Mexico the following morning. Taking in the view one last time. Happy for new connections, and friendships to have been formed. Sad to lose a few as well. Sometimes, the best moments are ones we don't want to believe. One thing I do believe is Bonnie Butterfield being the best woman for me. Detective Reisen jots down thoughts, and emotions in his journal. Peering out of the window, as the plane lands on a tarmac in chilly bittersweet Chicago.

Detective Reisen, and Bonnie Butterfield enter the bag pickup zone. Making their way outside, but not before a welcoming party is stationed awaiting them. Familiar faces, and new ones are present.

"Would you take a look at this," Detective Reisen states.

"Welcome back, old buddy," Detective Dewalt says.

He gives Detective Reisen, and Bonnie a hug.

"Happy to see each of you," Bonnie states.

"I have never been on a cruise, and I'm older than you. How was your trip?" Captain Davis inquires.

"We had fun," Bonnie interjects.

Everyone joins in for a laugh.

"We have a new face around here," Detective Reisen says.

"Nice to meet you, Detective Reisen. I am Suclese."

They shake hands, and everyone is in good spirits.

"Glad to meet you, and I'm excited to work with you, Suclese," Detective Reisen says.

Stepping forward is reelected Mayor Reinhart, accompanied by his security detail. Another man follows close behind. Detective Reisen hasn't met the new man yet.

"Glad the sharks didn't eat you alive," he jokes. "Bonnie, it's wonderful to see you. I bet you both were glued to the screen waiting for the results to come in!" Mayor Reinhart roars.

"I didn't watch the election results, because I didn't want to jinx you. Bonnie woke me up, and broke the good news to me," Detective Reisen confesses.

"Congratulations, Mayor Reinhart!" Bonnie commends.

"Thank you for the compliment, Detective, and thank you Bonnie," Mayor Reinhart says kissing Bonnie's hand.

That will cost you an exclusive interview," Bonnie states.

"You Betcha! First thing in the morning!" Mayor Reinhart confirms.

"Thank you!" Bonnie shouts.

Poking Mayor Reinhart's chest, "Smart of you to say yes to the lady," Detective Reisen jokes.

"I want you to meet somebody, Reisen." Mayor Reinhart pulls a man close, "This is City Prosecutor Scotch. He will be working closely with Progressive Task Force 12-Z."

Each member of Progressive Task Force 12-Z greets Mayor Reinhart, and City Prosecutor Scotch.

"Glad to see you all supporting your fellow officer. I bring good news, of course. Each one of you will be receiving a raise, and performance incentives!"

Bonnie turns around, and kisses Detective Reisen loud, and proud. Everyone cheers, and Captain Davis hugs Mayor Reinhart.

"This is all in appreciation of your dedication, and commitment to keeping the streets of Chicago safe."

"We can't thank you enough, Mayor Reinhart," Captain Davis says.

"I have already put the raises in through the proper channels. I made sure you are all compensated for the amazing work you are doing. I know this job is tough, but you are becoming tougher together."

"They should call you, the good mayor," Dewalt jokes.

"I wouldn't mind that," Mayor Reinhart admits.

Sharing a few laughs, and giggles before Mayor Reinhart ventures off.

"Don't say, I never did anything for you!" Mayor Reinhart shouts.

Mayor Reinhart, and his posse vanish faster than flint from a flick of a lighter.

"After you are situated at home, would you want to join us later on tonight?" Captain Davis asks.

"Swing by and pick me up. You can all fill me in on what's happening around here."

"Sounds good," Captain Davis states.

"For now, who wants to take us both home?" Bonnie asks.

"I will do the honors," Detective Dewalt offers.

After everyone splits up, Detective Dewalt makes certain Detective Reisen, and Bonnie arrive home safely.

"Did you forget about your best friend on the cruise?"

"Never. I have your souvenir right here, Dewalt."

Detective Reisen passes Detective Dewalt two free passes for a flight anywhere in the world. The passes he won from boxing Owana.

"Are you joking?" Detective Dewalt probes.

"I am an officer of the peace, not a comedian."

"Do I want to know where these came from?"

"Just understand, a man died so you may take that trip."

"Did you have to kill a man for these?" Dewalt probes.

"No. Unfortunately, he died later."

The City of Chicago is buzzing with excitement, but darkness is never far from sunshine. Unfinished business is a bad seed that will only harvest sorrow. Forces linger around unbound by complacency, and hellbent against transparency.

"Don't do anything stupid," Bonnie says.

She kisses Detective Reisen before he departs.

"The only thing stupid I could do would be lose you."

Entering in the back of Captain Davis's vehicle. Suclese rides in the passenger seat while, Detective Dewalt sits behind her.

"Good to see you all again," Detective Reisen states.

"We are extremely glad you are back," Dewalt insists.

"What is the latest information, besides Jake Frunk falling out of the picture?" Detective Reisen probes.

"Jake Frunk is not out of the picture," Captain Davis retorts.

"Oh! Wait, ... really? What happened?"

"We are investigating Jake Frunk for pushing a man off of a ledge," Suclese details.

"That's a huge leap," Detective Reisen responds.

They all quietly laugh under their breath.

"Don't worry the man was filthy rich. Dumber than dirt from what I could see," Detective Dewalt explains.

"Why do you believe he was dumb?" Reisen inquires.

"He invited Jake Frunk to his rooftop for dinner. No cameras or security were present," Captain Davis reveals.

"Who is this intellectual being?" Detective Reisen probes.

"Word from my informant is he is called the Golden One. They are still trying to figure out his true identity, down at the City Morgue," Detective Dewalt explains.

"Great work on the lead, team. Where does that lead us?" Detective Reisen inquires.

"We will have a good once over of who is at the Golden One's memorial service," Captain Davis states.

Driving a bit further when a billboard catches Detective Reisen's eyes. The billboard reads, Eric Greitens and Associates for Hire.

"Should say gang for hire," Detective Dewalt unloads.

Progressive Task Force 12-Z arrives at the Mount Isley Graveyard as the sun is setting.

"Detectives Reisen, and Dewalt head over to the opposite end. Take a good look at everyone's face. Suclese, roll with me," Captain Davis commands.

A draft in the room as the intensity of the moment takes shape.

"What do you mean the mayor, and city will need us?" Jake Frunk asks.

"Please, continue," Riley encourages.

"My privilege. I have obtained deeds to a handful of valuable properties in, and around Chicago. Two properties in particular are making huge money for the city in taxes, and tourism," Eric Greitens explains.

"Where do we fit in?" Jake Frunk probes.

"See, Jake. You are cleverer than at first glance. I'm going to take you both to view these two facilities. If you approve, then you will run the operations for the time being."

"What do you want from us in return?" Riley asks.

"Don't concern yourself with frivolous notions. This is a better offer than either of you have. You will be doing me a favor by allowing me to tie up some loose ends."

"Count me in," Jake Frunk confirms.

"I will play along ... for now," Riley says.

"This is exciting news! Let's not waste any daylight, and proceed right away," Greitens directs.

All three exit the safe house. Eric Greitens turns and locks the door. Entering Jake Frunk's vehicle and driving off into the distance. As the trio of trickery heads back into the City of Chicago, Progressive Task Force 12-Z continues their assignment.

"I knew drafting was my specialty when I chose you, Suclese," Captain Davis admonishes.

"Thank you, Captain Davis. What is your grand advice for me in the long run?"

"Consider a dollar valuable, and one minute as a lot of time. You will do just fine, and if you're open to the blessing from above ... a bit better," Captain Davis finishes.

Detective Suclese soaks up the free knowledge. Detectives Reisen and Dewalt look at the crowd of people set to bury the Golden One. Reisen notices a familiar face. Peering closer, Mr. Platinum is in mourning.

"The woman dressed in all black with purple gloves next to the elderly man is, Mindy. She's the only daughter of the deceased," Detective Dewalt details.

"Better known as the daughter of deceit," Captain Davis interjects.

Captain Davis and Suclese are standing with Detectives Dewalt and Reisen.

"Will Mindy be too much for us to handle?" Detective Reisen inquires.

"Let's hope not," Captain Davis replies.

"Does anyone notice a familiar face?" Dewalt probes.

"No. Nobody looks familiar," Detective Reisen states.

Don't miss out!

Visit the website below and you can sign up to receive emails whenever Preston Olson publishes a new book. There's no charge and no obligation.

https://books2read.com/r/B-A-XTTR-ZPLTC

BOOKS2READ

Connecting independent readers to independent writers.

Also by Preston Olson

Shields and Shadows
Badge in the Shadows
Smoke On The Cruise

Standalone
A Collection of Souls
The Green Guide

Watch for more at https://oddmanout.ninja.

About the Author

Author of Badge in the Shadows, Three Down, and more! Music on all streaming services under Heavy P. Love coffee, the Green Bay Packers, and nature!

Read more at https://oddmanout.ninja.